EYES WIDE SHUT

EYES WIDE SHUT

A Screenplay by Stanley Kubrick and Frederic Raphael

AND

the Classic Novel That Inspired the Film
Dream Story by Arthur Schnitzler

WARNER BOOKS

A Time Warner Company

Cover photograph copyright © 1999 by Warner Bros.
Screenplay copyright © 1999 by Warner Bros.
Traumnovelle first published in German, 1926; English translation copyright © 1999 by J.M.Q. Davies
Compilation copyright © 1999 by Warner Books, Inc.
Interior photographs copyright © 1999 by Warner Bros.
All rights reserved.

Warner Books, Inc., 1271 Avenue of the Americas, New York, NY 10020

Visit our Web site at www.twbookmark.com

 A Time Warner Company

Printed in the United States of America

First Printing: October 1999

10 9 8 7 6 5 4 3 2 1

ISBN: 0-446-67632-2
LCCN: 99-64443

Book design by Stanley S. Drate / Folio Graphics Company, Inc.

EYES WIDE SHUT

FADE IN:

FIRST CARD:

TOM CRUISE

SECOND CARD:

NICOLE KIDMAN

THIRD CARD:

A FILM BY STANLEY KUBRICK

1. INT. DRESSING ROOM – BILL & ALICE'S
APARTMENT – NIGHT

*ALICE, a beautiful woman with her back to CAMERA,
lets drop an elegant black dress to the floor.*

MAIN TITLE CARD:

EYES WIDE SHUT

2. EXT. APARTMENT BLOCK – NEW YORK – NIGHT

BILL and ALICE's apartment block on Central Park West.

3. INT. DRESSING ROOM – BILL & ALICE'S
APARTMENT – NIGHT

A handsome man in evening dress is looking for something. He walks into a bedroom, goes to a small table, picks up keys and a mobile phone and walks to a chest of drawers. This is Bill Harford, a doctor.
  Bill opens a drawer and takes out a handkerchief.

> BILL
> Honey, have you seen my wallet?

> ALICE *(o/s)*
> Ah . . . isn't it on the bedside table?

BILL walks across to the bedside table and finds his wallet.

> BILL
> Ah, yep . . . now listen, you know we're running
> a little late?

BILL goes around the bed and into the en-suite bathroom. ALICE is sitting on the loo wearing an evening dress.

ALICE

I know. How do I look?

BILL goes to the mirror to check his appearance without looking at ALICE.

BILL

Perfect.

ALICE gets up from the loo as BILL checks his bow tie.

ALICE

Is my hair OK?

BILL

It's great.

ALICE drops the toilet tissue in the loo and flushes it away.

ALICE

You're not even looking at it.

BILL turns and looks at her adoringly.

BILL

It's beautiful.

BILL kisses her affectionately on the cheek and leaves the bathroom.

                    BILL
You always look beautiful.

                    ALICE
Did you give Roz the phone and pager numbers?

                  BILL *(o/s)*
Yeah. I put it on the fridge . . . let's go, huh?

*ALICE washes her hands and dries them as she looks in
the mirror.*

                    ALICE
Good. All right, I'm ready.

*ALICE removes her glasses, leaves the bathroom and
goes to the bed to pick up her coat and bag. BILL, his
overcoat on his arm, switches off the music centre. They
leave the bedroom together. BILL switches off the lights.*

4. INT. CORRIDOR – BILL & ALICE'S APARTMENT –
NIGHT

*BILL and ALICE walk down the corridor. ALICE starts
to put her coat on and BILL helps her.*

                    BILL
What's the name of the baby sitter?

ALICE
(whispering)

Roz.

They enter a spacious and comfortably furnished living room where HELENA, their seven-year-old daughter, sits watching television with ROZ, the student baby sitter. There is a decorated Christmas tree behind the sofa.

ALICE
OK, Roz. We're going now.

ROZ
(standing)
Wow! You look amazing, Mrs Harford!

ALICE
Oh, thank you . . . Helena, are you ready for bed?

BILL puts on his overcoat.

HELENA
Yes, mummy. Can I stay up and watch *The Nutcracker*?

ALICE
What time's it on?

> HELENA

Nine o'clock.

> ALICE

Sure, you can watch that.

> HELENA

Can I stay up until you get home?

> ALICE

No, darling.

> BILL
> *(kissing Helena)*

It's going to be a little late for that.

> ALICE
> *(to Roz)*

Now, the phone number is on the fridge. . . .

ALICE bends down to kiss HELENA.

> ROZ

OK.

> ALICE

And there's plenty of food in there, so help
yourself.

ROZ

OK.

ALICE

We shouldn't be home any later than one
o'clock.

BILL

I'll hold our cab tonight to take you home.

ROZ

Thanks, Dr Harford.

ALICE
(to Helena)

You be a good baby.

HELENA

Good night, mummy. Good night, daddy.
Goodbye . . . bye.

ROZ

Have fun.

*BILL and ALICE leave, blowing kisses and waving bye-
bye to HELENA.*

ALICE
(to Helena)
See you in the morning.

BILL and ALICE walk down the apartment corridor.

5. EXT. ZIEGLER MANSION – NEW YORK – NIGHT

A palatial house in mid-town Manhattan. Doormen stand outside the entrance. A large stretch limo is parked nearby.

6. INT. CORRIDOR – ZIEGLER MANSION – NIGHT

BILL and ALICE, holding hands, walk down a corridor lined with display cases and works of art. A large party is in progress. Guests, all in evening wear, are still arriving. An orchestra playing dance music can be heard further off in the house.

BILL and ALICE come into a large hallway where their hosts, Victor ZIEGLER and his wife, ILONA, are greeting the guests to their annual Christmas party.

BILL
Victor, Ilona. . . .

ZIEGLER *(o/s)*
Bill, Alice. . . .

The hall is large and marbled with a vast staircase in the background. Illuminations creating a "curtain of light" hang from the walls and there is a Christmas tree laden with decorations. ZIEGLER, a fit, sun-tanned man in his fifties, and his beautiful wife welcome BILL and ALICE.

BILL

Merry Christmas!

ZIEGLER

Merry Christmas! How good to see both of you. Thanks so much for coming.

ALICE

We wouldn't have missed it for the world.

ZIEGLER

Alice, look at you! God, you're absolutely stunning.

ALICE

Oh, thank you.

ZIEGLER
(to Ilona)
And I don't say that to all the women, do I?

ILONA

Oh, yes, he does.

ALICE

He does!

ZIEGLER

(to Bill)

Hey, that osteopath you sent me to got to work
on my arm . . . you should see my serve now,
it's terrific!

BILL

He's the top man in New York.

ZIEGLER

I could have told you that looking at his bill.
Listen, go inside, have a drink, enjoy the party
and I'll see you in a little bit. OK? Thanks for
coming.

BILL

Thank you.

ALICE

Bye.

*BILL and ALICE make their way to the crowded main
reception room.*

7. INT. BALLROOM – ZIEGLER MANSION – NIGHT

*The walls are draped with the "curtain of light" illumi-
nations seen in the corridor. There is a stage and upon*

it is the small orchestra playing ballroom music. The guests dance on the crowded floor. BILL and ALICE dance together.

ALICE

Do you know anyone here?

BILL

Not a soul.

ALICE

Why do you think Ziegler invites us to these things every year?

BILL

This is what you get for making house calls.

On the stage there is a young man of similar age to BILL playing the piano. He is dressed in a white tux and bow tie. He looks around. This is NICK Nightingale. BILL notices him.

BILL
(to Alice)
You see that guy at the piano? I went to medical school with him.

ALICE
Really? He plays pretty good for a doctor.

> BILL

He's not a doctor. He dropped out.

The bandleader brings the music to a stop.

> BANDLEADER

Ladies and gentlemen, I hope you're enjoying yourselves. The band is going to take a short break now and we'll be back in ten minutes.

The guests applaud as the band leaves the stage.

> BILL
> *(indicating Nick)*

Let's go over and say hello to him.

> ALICE

Honey, I desperately need to go to the bathroom. You go and say hello and I'll meet you . . . where? At the bar?

> BILL

Good.

BILL kisses ALICE on the cheek as she leaves the ballroom.

8. INT. ANTE-ROOM – ZIEGLER MANSION – NIGHT

Crowded with guests. ALICE walks by a waiter holding a tray with glasses of champagne. She takes a glass without stopping and drinks it "in one" as she moves away.

9. INT. BALLROOM – ZIEGLER MANSION – NIGHT

On stage, by the piano, Nick Nightingale sorts through some sheet music as the band takes its break. Bill walks up to the stage.

BILL
Nightingale! Nick Nightingale!

NICK looks around to see who is calling his name. He jumps down from the stage and he and BILL greet each other like old friends.

NICK
Oh, my God! Bill! Bill Harford! How the hell are you, buddy?

BILL
How long has it been?

NICK
Oh, jeez! I don't know, about ten years?

BILL
And a couple. Do you have time for a drink?

                    NICK

Sure.

*BILL puts his arm round NICK's shoulders as they walk
to the other end of the ballroom.*

                    BILL

God, you haven't changed a bit!

                    NICK

Thanks, I *think*. So how you doing?

                    BILL

Not too bad, you know, not too bad. I see you've
become a pianist.

                    NICK

Oh, yes. Well my friends call me that. How
about you? You still in the doctor business?

                    BILL

You know what they say, once a doctor always
a doctor.

*BILL takes a couple of glasses of champagne from a
waiter standing with a tray and hands one to NICK.*

                    NICK

Yes, or in my case, never a doctor, never a
doctor.

                    BILL
I never did understand why you walked away.

                    NICK
No? It's a nice feeling. I do it a lot. Cheers.

They "clink" glasses as a man in evening dress walks up to NICK. This is ZIEGLER's SECRETARY.

                  SECRETARY
Excuse me . . . Nick, I need you a minute.

                    NICK
Be right with you.
                  (to Bill)
Listen, I gotta go do something. If I don't catch you later, I'm gonna be down the Village for two weeks in a place called the Sonata café. Stop by if you get a chance.

                    BILL
I'll be there. Great seeing you.

                    NICK
Good seeing you too.

They exchange friendly pats as Nick goes.

10. INT. ANTE-ROOM – ZIEGLER MANSION –
NIGHT

ALICE stands, back to the bar, holding a glass of champagne. The room is crowded with people talking. A tall, handsome man, suave and middle-aged, also stands at the bar. He turns from a conversation he is having and notices ALICE next to him. His name is Sandor SZAVOST. He takes a sip of whisky as he studies her, and puts his glass down on the bar. ALICE, still looking for BILL to join her, also puts her champagne glass down.

SZAVOST then nonchalantly picks ALICE's glass up as ALICE turns to do the same.

                    ALICE
Umm, I . . . I think that's *my* glass.

                    SZAVOST
I'm absolutely certain of it.

SZAVOST stares into ALICE's eyes as he seductively drinks the contents of ALICE's glass.

                    SZAVOST
My name is Sandor Szavost. I'm Hungarian.

He takes Alice's hand and kisses it.

                    ALICE
                (a little tipsy)
My name is Alice Harford. I'm American.

SZAVOST

Delighted to meet you, Alice. Did you ever read
the Latin poet Ovid on *The Art of Love*?

ALICE

Didn't he wind up all by himself? Crying his
eyes out in some place with a very bad climate?

SZAVOST

But he also had a good time first, a *very* good
time. Are you here with anyone tonight, Alice?

ALICE

With my husband.

SZAVOST

Oh, how sad! But then I'm sure he's the sort of
man who wouldn't mind if we danced.

*ALICE thinks for a moment then offers her arm to
SZAVOST.*

11. INT. BALLROOM – ZIEGLER MANSION – NIGHT

SZAVOST and ALICE dance closely on the crowded floor.

SZAVOST

What do you do, Alice?

ALICE

Well, at the moment I am looking for a job. I
used to manage an art gallery in Soho but it
went broke.

(giggles)

SZAVOST

Oh, what a shame! I have some friends in the
art game. Perhaps they can be of some help?

ALICE

Oh, thank you.

*As they turn, ALICE catches sight of BILL talking to two
beautiful girls in the ante-room beyond.*

SZAVOST

Someone you know?

ALICE

My husband.

SZAVOST

Oh. Don't you think one of the charms of
marriage is that it makes deception a necessity
for both parties?

ALICE laughs.

                    SZAVOST
May I ask why a beautiful women who could
have any man in this room wants to be
married?

                    ALICE
Why wouldn't she?

                    SZAVOST
Is it as bad as that?

                    ALICE
As good as that.

12. INT. ANTE-ROOM – ZIEGLER MANSION –
NIGHT

*The two beautiful girls, GAYLE and NUALA, have their
arms draped around each other as they talk to BILL.*

                    GAYLE
Do you know Nuala Windsor?

                    BILL
No, no. And it's very, very lovely to meet you
both.

They all laugh.

> BILL

How do you spell Nuala?

> NUALA

N . . . U . . . A . . . L . . . A.

> GAYLE

You don't remember me, do you?

BILL tries to think.

> GAYLE

You were very kind to me once.

> BILL

Only once? That sounds like a terrible
oversight!

> GAYLE

I was doing a photo session in Rockefeller
Plaza, on a very windy day.

> BILL

And you got something in your eye?

> GAYLE

Just about half of Fifth Avenue.

BILL

Right.

GAYLE

You were such a gentleman, you gave me your
handkerchief, which was also clean.

BILL

Well that is the kind of hero I can be . . .
sometimes.

13. INT. BALLROOM – ZIEGLER MANSION – NIGHT

ALICE and SZAVOST continue dancing.

SZAVOST

You know why women used to get married,
don't you?

ALICE

Why don't you tell me?

SZAVOST

It was the only way they could lose their
virginity *and* be free to do what they wanted
with other men . . . the ones they really wanted.

ALICE

Fascinating.

14. INT. ANOTHER CORRIDOR – ZIEGLER
MANSION – NIGHT

*GAYLE and NUALA walk on each side of BILL, their
arms linked through his.*

GAYLE

Do you know what's so nice about doctors?

BILL

Usually a lot less than people imagine.

GAYLE

They always seem so knowledgeable.

BILL

Oh, they are very knowledgeable about all sorts
of things.

GAYLE

But I bet they work too hard. Just think of all
they miss.

BILL

You're probably right. Now, where exactly are
we going . . . exactly?

They come into a large room where there are few people.

> GAYLE

Where the rainbow ends?

> BILL

Where the rainbow ends?

They come to a stop.

> NUALA

Don't you want to go where the rainbow ends?

> BILL

Well, now that depends where that is.

> GAYLE

Well, let's find out.

A tall good looking man walks up to them and interrupts. He is HARRIS, ZIEGLER's personal assistant.

> HARRIS

Excuse me, ladies.
> > *(to Bill)*

Sorry, Dr Harford. Sorry to interrupt. I wonder whether you could come with me for a moment? Something for Mr Ziegler.

> BILL

Oh . . . umm . . . Fine.
> > *(to the two girls)*

To be continued?

HARRIS leads BILL across the hall and up the marble staircase.

15. INT. BATHROOM – ZIEGLER MANSION – NIGHT

ZIEGLER hurriedly pulls his trousers up while looking down on a girl lying unconscious and naked in an armchair. This is MANDY who is making quiet muttering noises. ZIEGLER is panic stricken. He hears a knock on the door and runs barefoot across the bathroom to open it.

ZIEGLER
Yeah?

He opens the door to see BILL standing there with HARRIS. He shakes BILL's hand.

ZIEGLER
Bill, thank God.

ZIEGLER closes the door, leaving HARRIS outside to keep watch.

ZIEGLER
We had a . . . had a little accident here.

They walk over to MANDY.

BILL

What happened?

BILL takes a closer look at MANDY.

ZIEGLER

Well, she . . . she was shooting up and she . . .
she had a bad reaction.

BILL

(feels Mandy's pulse)

What did she take?

ZIEGLER

Speedball or snowball or whatever the hell they
call it. You know, it's . . . it's heroin and coke.

BILL

Heroin and coke . . . uh-huh. Anything else?

ZIEGLER

Ah, yeah, a couple of drinks. Nothing really.
Some champagne. That was it.

BILL

How long's she been like this?

ZIEGLER

Maybe five minutes, six minutes. Something
like that.

> BILL

What's her name?

> ZIEGLER

Mandy . . . Mandy.

MANDY continues making quiet, muttering noises.

> BILL

Mandy. Mandy. Can you hear me, Mandy? Can
you hear me? Just move your head for me if you
can hear me. Just move your head for me if you
can hear me, Mandy. There you go, you can
hear me. Can you open your eyes for me?
Mandy? Can you do that? Let me see you do
that. Let me see you open your eyes. There you
go. Come on, come on. Look at me, look at me,
look at me, look at me. Look at me. Look at me,
Mandy. Good. Good.

16. INT. BALLROOM – ZIEGLER MANSION – NIGHT

*SZAVOST and ALICE are still dancing. ALICE is quite in-
toxicated by both SZAVOST and the champagne.*

> SZAVOST

I love Victor's art collection, don't you?

> ALICE

Yes . . . it's wonderful.

SZAVOST

Have you ever seen his sculpture gallery?

ALICE

No, I haven't.

SZAVOST

He has a wonderful collection of Renaissance
bronzes. Do you like the period?

ALICE

Hmm . . . I do.

SZAVOST

I adore it. The sculpture gallery is upstairs.
Would you like to see it? I can show it to you.
We won't be gone long.

ALICE

Maybe . . . not just . . . now.

17. INT. BATHROOM – ZIEGLER MANSION – NIGHT

*ZIEGLER, now dressed in his shirt, does his cufflinks up.
BILL leans up against a sideboard, arms folded, watching MANDY. She is still in the chair, but she is now covered with a blue bathrobe. ZIEGLER stands over her.*

> ZIEGLER
> Well, that was really one hell of a scare you
> gave us, kiddo.

> MANDY
> Sorry.

> BILL
> How are you feeling now, Mandy?

> MANDY
> Better.

BILL goes over to her and kneels down.

> BILL
> You are a very, very lucky girl. You know that?

> MANDY
> I know.

> BILL
> You're going to be OK this time, but you can't
> keep doing this. You understand?

> MANDY
> Yeah.

> BILL

You're going to need some rehab. You know
that, don't you?

> MANDY

I know.

> BILL

OK . . . OK.

BILL gets up and turns to ZIEGLER.

> BILL

Well, Victor, I think I can leave the rest to you.

> ZIEGLER

Is it OK if I get some clothes on her and get her
out of here?

> BILL

No. I'd . . . I'd keep her here for another hour.

> ZIEGLER

Another hour?

> BILL

I'd have someone take her home.

                    ZIEGLER

OK . . . OK.

They walk towards the door.

                    BILL

Goodnight, Mandy.

                    ZIEGLER

Listen, I can't thank you enough for this. You
saved my ass.

                    BILL

I'm glad I was here.

                    ZIEGLER

Bill . . . I probably . . . I know I don't have to
mention this, but this is just between us. OK?

                    BILL

Of course.

18. INT. BALLROOM – ZIEGLER MANSION – NIGHT

*ALICE, eyes shut, dances closely to SZAVOST, as if in a
trance. She brings herself "to" as they stop dancing.*

                    ALICE

I think I've had a little too much champagne. I
think I have to go and find my husband now.

SZAVOST

I'm sure he'll be all right on his own a little
longer.

ALICE

Yes, but will *I*?

SZAVOST

Of course you will.

ALICE

No, no, no, I . . . I really have to go. I have to go.

SZAVOST

You don't, you know.

ALICE

Yes, I do.

SZAVOST

Alice, I must see you again.

ALICE

That's impossible.

SZAVOST

Why?

ALICE

Because . . . I'm married.

ALICE waves her ring finger in front of SZAVOST's face. She kisses her index finger and plants it on SZAVOST's lips as she leaves him on the dance floor.

19. INT. BEDROOM – BILL & ALICE'S APARTMENT – NIGHT

ALICE stands naked in front of the bedroom mirror. She removes an ear-ring as she sways around. As she begins to take the other ear-ring off BILL comes up behind her and starts to caress her. He puts his arms around her and lovingly touches her. She responds to his caresses by taking her glasses off and putting her arms around him. They kiss. ALICE looks at herself in the mirror as BILL kisses her neck and shoulder.

20. INT. RECEPTION – BILL'S SURGERY – DAY

The lift doors open and BILL steps out.

BILL

Good morning, Lisa.

LISA

Good morning, doctor. Your mail.

                    BILL
Good. Please ask Janelle if she will bring me my
coffee.

                    LISA
Sure.

BILL walks through the reception towards his office.

                    BILL
Thank you. Good morning, Sarah.

                    SARAH
Good morning, doctor.

21. INT. KITCHEN – BILL & ALICE'S APARTMENT –
DAY

*ALICE sits reading the morning paper and drinking her
coffee dressed in a morning gown. HELENA, still in her
night clothes, eats breakfast while watching television.*

22. INT. EXAMINATION ROOM – BILL'S SURGERY –
DAY

*BILL examines a young woman's chest using a stetho-
scope. His female nurse stands by as an observer.*

                    BILL
OK. That's fine. You can put your gown on.

23. INT. HELENA'S BEDROOM – BILL & ALICE'S APARTMENT – DAY

HELENA, in a red dress and jumper, is having her hair brushed by ALICE, still in her morning gown.
  ALICE then gives HELENA the brush.

ALICE

Hold. . . .

HELENA takes the brush as ALICE arranges her daughter's hair in a pony tail.

24. INT. EXAMINATION ROOM – BILL'S SURGERY – DAY

BILL examines a young boy's neck glands as his mother waits in the background.

BILL

Looking forward to Christmas?

BOY

Yeah.

BILL

Does this hurt?

BOY

Yeah.

25. INT. DRESSING ROOM – BILL & ALICE'S
APARTMENT – DAY

ALICE is naked. She puts on a bra.

26. INT. EXAMINATION ROOM – BILL'S SURGERY –
DAY

*BILL, with female nurse in attendance, examines a man
who lies on the table. He pulls the patient's leg gently
upwards.*

                    BILL
      Right there?

                    PATIENT
      Yeah.

27. INT. BATHROOM – BILL & ALICE'S
APARTMENT – DAY

*ALICE, in skirt and bra, rolls deodorant under her arms
as HELENA cleans her teeth.*

28. INT. LIVING ROOM – BILL & ALICE'S
APARTMENT – DAY

*ALICE and HELENA wrap Christmas presents on the
table.*

                    ALICE
        Oh, daddy's gonna like that . . . a very good
        choice.

29. INT. HELENA'S BEDROOM – BILL & ALICE'S
APARTMENT – NIGHT

*BILL and ALICE sit with HELENA as she reads from her
picture book, ALICE prompting her as BILL watches and
listens.*

                    HELENA
        Before me, when I jump into my bed.

30. INT. LIVING ROOM – BILL & ALICE'S
APARTMENT – NIGHT

*ALICE walks by the dining table as she goes to the sitting
room. She yawns as she goes.*

                    ALICE
        I should call the Zieglers and thank them for the
        party last night.

                    BILL
        I've taken care of that.

*BILL sits on the sofa watching a football game on televi-
sion. ALICE joins him.*

ALICE

So how do you feel about wrapping the rest of
the presents?

BILL

(hesitates)

Oh, oh . . . let's do that tomorrow.

31. INT. BATHROOM – BILL & ALICE'S APARTMENT
– NIGHT

*ALICE, tired, looks into the mirror of the bathroom cabi-
net. She opens it up and takes out a Band-Aid tin. She
opens the tin and removes a packet of cigarette papers
and a polythene bag of grass (marijuana). She leaves the
bathroom.*

32. INT. BEDROOM – BILL & ALICE'S
APARTMENT – NIGHT

ALICE rolls a joint.

33. INT. BEDROOM – BILL & ALICE'S
APARTMENT – NIGHT

*ALICE, lying on the bed in her underwear, takes a "pull"
on the joint. She passes the spliff to BILL, who sits on the
bed next to her dressed only in boxer shorts.*

ALICE

Hmm . . . tell me something . . . those two girls
at the party last night. Did you, by any chance,
happen to fuck them?

BILL

(coughs and splutters)
What!? What are you talking about!?

ALICE

I'm talking about the two girls that you were so
blatantly hitting on.

BILL

I wasn't hitting on anybody.

ALICE

Hmm . . . Who were they?

BILL

They were just a couple of models.

ALICE sits up next to BILL.

ALICE

And where did you disappear to with them for
so long?

BILL starts to kiss and touch ALICE.

BILL

Ohhhh! Wait a minute, wait a minute! I didn't
disappear with anybody. Ziegler wasn't feeling
too well. I got called upstairs to see him.
Anyway, who's the guy you were dancing with?

ALICE
(laughs)
A friend of the Zieglers'.

BILL

What did he want?

ALICE
(as Bill kisses her ear)
What did *he* want? Oh . . . what did he want?
Sex – upstairs, then and there.

BILL

Is that all?

ALICE
Yeah . . . yeah. That was all.

BILL
(kissing Alice)
Just wanted to fuck my wife.

ALICE
(giggles)
Yeah, that's right.

BILL
I guess that's understandable.

ALICE
(suddenly serious)
Understandable?

BILL
Because you are a very, very beautiful woman.

ALICE
Woah! Woah! Woah! Wait!

ALICE puts the spliff into the ashtray on the bed, disengages herself from BILL's arms, and gets up. She backs up towards the bathroom leaving BILL sitting on the bed.

ALICE
So . . . because I'm a beautiful woman the only reason any man wants to talk to me is because he wants to fuck me! Is that what you're saying?

BILL
Well, I don't think it's quite that black and

white, but I think we both know what men are
like.

ALICE now leans against the door frame.

ALICE
So, on that basis I should conclude that you
wanted to fuck those two models?

BILL
There are exceptions.

ALICE
What makes you an exception?

BILL
What makes me an exception is that . . . I
happen to be in love with you and because
we're married and because I would never lie to
you or hurt you.

ALICE starts walking to the other end of the room.

ALICE
Do you realize that what you're saying is that
the only reason you wouldn't fuck those two
models is out of consideration for me, not
because you really wouldn't want to?

BILL

Let's just relax, Alice. This pot is making you aggressive.

ALICE

No, it's not the pot, it's you! Why can't you ever give me a straight fucking answer!

BILL

I was under the impression that's what I was doing. I don't even know what we're arguing about here.

ALICE

(sits on a stool)

I'm not arguing. I'm just trying to find out where you're coming from.

BILL

Where I'm coming from?

ALICE gets up and stands at the end of the bed.

ALICE

Let's say, let's say for example, you have some gorgeous woman standing in your office naked and you're feeling her fucking tits. Now, what I wanna know . . . I wanna know what are you really thinking about when you're squeezing them?

BILL

Alice, I happen to be a doctor. It's all very impersonal and you know there is always a nurse present.

ALICE

So, when you are feeling tits it's nothing more than your professionalism, is that what you're saying?

BILL

Exactly . . . sex is the last thing on my mind when I'm with a patient.

ALICE

Now, when she is having her little titties squeezed, do you think she ever has any little fantasies about what handsome Doctor Bill's dickie might be like?

BILL

Come on, I can assure you that sex is the last thing on this fucking hypothetical woman patient's mind.

ALICE

And what makes you so sure?

BILL

If for no better reason . . . because she's afraid of what I might find.

ALICE

OK! OK! So, so, so after you tell her that
everything's fine, what then?

BILL

What then? Ah, I don't know that, Alice. *What
then?* Look, women don't . . . they basically
don't think like that.

*ALICE gets up and provocatively points a finger at BILL
as she starts to pace up and down at the foot of the bed.*

ALICE

Millions of years of evolution, right? Right?
Men have to stick it in every place they can, but
for women . . . women it is just about security
and commitment and whatever the fuck . . .
else!

BILL

A little oversimplified, Alice, but yes, something
like that.

ALICE

If you men only knew. . . .

BILL

I'll tell you what I do know is that you got a
little stoned tonight. You've been trying to pick

a fight with me and now you're trying to make
me jealous.

ALICE

But you're not the jealous type, are you?

BILL

No, I'm not.

ALICE

You've never been jealous about me, have you?

BILL

No, I haven't.

ALICE

And why haven't you ever been jealous about
me?

BILL

Well, I don't know, Alice. Maybe because you're
my wife, maybe because you're the mother of
my child and I know you would never be
unfaithful to me.

ALICE

You are very, very sure of yourself, aren't you?

BILL

No, I'm sure of *you*.

ALICE bursts out laughing.

BILL

Do you think that's funny?

ALICE collapses onto the floor, her laughing fit uncontrollable now.

BILL

Fucking laughing fit, right?

ALICE calms down a little.

ALICE

Do you . . . do you remember last summer at Cape Cod?

BILL

Yes.

ALICE

Do you remember one night in the dining room? There was this young naval officer and he was sitting near our table with two other officers?

ALICE sits back against the radiator and focuses on her story.

BILL

No.

ALICE

The waiter brought him a message at which
point he left. Nothing rings a bell?

BILL

No.

ALICE

Well, I first saw him that morning in the lobby.
He was . . . he was checking into the hotel and
he was following the bell-boy with his luggage,
to the elevator. He . . . he glanced at me as he
walked past, just a glance. Nothing more. But I
could hardly move. That afternoon Helena
went to the movies with her friend and you and
I made love, and we made plans about our
future and we talked about Helena and yet at
no time was he ever out of my mind. And I
thought if he wanted me, even if it was for only
one night, I was ready to give up everything.
You, Helena, my whole fucking future.
Everything. And yet it was weird because at the
same time you were dearer to me than ever and
. . . and at that moment my love for you was
both tender and sad. I . . . I barely slept that
night and I woke up the next morning in a
panic. I didn't know whether I was afraid he

had left or that he might still be there, but by
dinner I realized he was gone and I was
relieved.

*BILL is stunned by what ALICE is telling him and it is
some time before he can respond to the repeated ringing
of the telephone. He finally picks it up.*

> BILL
>
> Hello? Yes, this is Dr Harford. When did it
> happen? No, no, erh . . . I have the address.
> Thank you.
>
> *(to Alice)*
>
> Lou Nathanson just died. I'm gonna have to go
> over there and show my face.

34. INT. TAXI CAB – NIGHT

*BILL sits in the cab thinking about what ALICE has told
him.*

35. INT. ROOM – CAPE COD – DAY

*BILL, in his jealousy, fantasises about ALICE and the
NAVAL OFFICER making love.*

36. INT. TAXI CAB – NIGHT

BILL continues to torture himself with ALICE's confession.

37. INT. LOBBY – NATHANSON APARTMENT
BUILDING – NIGHT

The elevator door opens and BILL comes out. He walks across the elegant, art deco lobby and presses a door-bell.

38. INT. HALLWAY – NATHANSON APARTMENT –
NIGHT

A maid walks to the door of the luxurious apartment and peeps through the spy-hole. This is ROSA. She opens the door.

> BILL

Good evening, Rosa.

> ROSA

Good evening, Dr Harford.

> BILL

How is Miss Nathanson?

> ROSA

Not so good. She's in the bedroom.

> BILL

Thank you.

BILL walks down the hallway, passing numerous objets d'art and paintings and comes to a door. He knocks.

MARION *(o/s)*

Come in.

BILL goes into the room.

39. INT. BEDROOM – NATHANSON APARTMENT – NIGHT

BILL comes into the bedroom and is greeted by a beautiful woman in her late thirties. This is MARION Nathanson who is crying over the loss of her father.

BILL

Marion.

MARION

Oh! Dr Harford! How . . . how good of you to come.

BILL

I came as soon as I got the message.

MARION

Oh, thank you.

                         BILL
I'm so . . . I'm so sorry.

                        MARION
Oh, thank you.

                         BILL
Your father was a . . . was a very brave man.

                        MARION
Oh, thank you.

                         BILL
How are you holding up?

                        MARION
Ah . . . ah . . . I'm a bit numb. I don't think it's
really sunk in yet. Erh, would you like to sit
down?

*BILL walks around the bed and up to the dead body of
LOU NATHANSON. BILL puts his hand on the corpse's
forehead and then he and MARION move to a table and
chairs nearby and sit down.*

                        MARION
It's so unreal. Daddy had such a good day. His
mind was clear and he remembered so many
things and then he had a little dinner and he

said he felt like taking a nap. I . . . I went into
the kitchen and talked to Rosa for half an hour
at most and when I went back in to see how he
was I just thought he was asleep and then I . . .
then I realized he wasn't breathing.

BILL

Marion, from what you've said, I'm sure your
father died peacefully in his sleep.

MARION

Oh, God! I hope so! I think I've been more afraid
of the way it was actually going to happen than
his death itself.

BILL

Have you had a chance to phone any of your
relatives?

MARION

I umm . . . I tried to call my step-mother in
London but, erh, she was out. My boyfriend,
Carl, is making some calls and umm, he'll be
coming over soon. I think you've met Carl here
a few times?

BILL

Yes, I remember him. He's a teacher isn't he?

MARION

A maths professor. We're going to get married
in May.

BILL

Well, that's wonderful news. Congratulations.

MARION

Thank you. Carl has a new teaching
appointment at the University of Michigan.
We'll be moving out there soon.

BILL

Well, Michigan is a beautiful state. I think
you'll like it a lot.

MARION

(starting to break)

Yeah.

BILL

It really could be a wonderful change for you,
Marion.

MARION

I . . . oh! No. I . . . Oh, my God! No! I . . . I love
you. I love you. I love you. I love you.

MARION tries to control herself, but she finally breaks down. She looks at BILL in desperation then moves forward to kiss him passionately on his lips.

BILL

Marion.

MARION

I love you. I don't want to go away with Carl.

BILL

Marion, I don't think you realize. . . .

MARION

I do, even if I'm never to see you again, I want at least to live near you.

BILL

Marion, listen to me, listen to me. You're very upset right now and I don't think you realize what you're saying.

MARION

I love you.

BILL

We barely know each other. I don't think we've had a single conversation about anything except your father.

MARION

I love you.

The sound of the door chimes is heard.

MARION

Oh, that's probably Carl. Please don't despise me.

She gets up, leaving BILL to sit and ponder what has happened.

40. INT. HALLWAY – NATHANSON APARTMENT – NIGHT

ROSA opens the door to a studious-looking man in glasses. This is CARL, MARION's fiancé. He hands ROSA his coat and scarf.

CARL

Hello, Rosa.

ROSA

Hello, Mr Thomas.

CARL

Is she . . . is she in the bedroom?

ROSA

Yes, she is.

>   CARL
> Thank you.

CARL walks down the corridor and comes to the bedroom door. He knocks.

>   MARION *(o/s)*
> Come in.

41. INT. BEDROOM – NATHANSON APARTMENT –
NIGHT

CARL enters and walks across to MARION. They kiss.

>   CARL
> Darling, I'm so very sorry. Are you all right?

>   MARION
> I'm OK.

CARL walks over to BILL and they shake hands.

>   CARL
> Dr Harford, good evening.

>   BILL
> Good evening, Carl.

                        CARL

Thank you very much for coming over here
tonight.

                        BILL

It's the least I could do.

                        CARL

It means a lot to us.

                        BILL

Thank you.
                      (pause)
Well, I, I was actually on my way out.
                    (to Marion)
Marion, your father was very proud of you and
I know you gave him great comfort these last
months.

                       MARION

Thank you.

                        CARL

Thank you.

                        BILL

Well. . . .

CARL

Well . . . I'll show you out.

BILL

Good night.

CARL shows BILL out and MARION is left in a state of confusion.

42. EXT. STREET – GREENWICH VILLAGE – NIGHT

Cabs, night life, a few pedestrians.

43. EXT. ANOTHER STREET – GREENWICH VILLAGE – NIGHT

BILL walks aimlessly along the street. He sees a young couple up against a shop front kissing passionately, oblivious of all around them.

44. INT. ROOM – CAPE COD – DAY

The taunting fantasy image of ALICE and the NAVAL OFFICER making love returns to haunt BILL.

45. EXT. ANOTHER STREET – GREENWICH VILLAGE – NIGHT

BILL continues walking, beating his fists in anger over his fantasy. He turns a corner and sees a gang of rowdy college boys coming towards him. The six of them take up the whole sidewalk.

STUDENT 1
I'm serious, I got scars on the back of my neck.

They notice BILL and start to hurl insults at him.

STUDENT 2
Hey! Hey! Hey! Hey! What team's this we're trying to play for?

STUDENT 1
Looks like the pink team!

BILL moves aside to avoid them, but as they pass, one of them deliberately elbows him up against a car parked by the sidewalk. BILL falls but regains his balance. The students start to insult him, provocatively taunting him about his sexuality. BILL stands and angrily stares at them then, as they continue down the street shouting their insults, he finally turns and walks on.

46. EXT. ANOTHER STREET – GREENWICH VILLAGE – NIGHT

BILL continues on his way, hands deep in pockets, mind deep in thought. He comes to a street crossing where he has to wait before continuing. He is approached by a young girl, dressed in a fun-fur coat and hat. This is DOMINO.

> DOMINO
> Excuse me, do you know what time it is?

> BILL
> Ten past twelve.

> DOMINO
> Going anywhere special?

> BILL
> *(a little annoyed)*
> No, I'm just . . . just taking a walk.

He starts to cross the street and the girl falls in step alongside him.

> DOMINO
> How'd you like to have a little fun?

> BILL
> I'm . . . I'm sorry?

> DOMINO
> A little fun? I just live right down there.

She indicates a house farther down the street.

DOMINO

Would you like to come inside with me?

BILL

Come inside with you?

DOMINO

Yeah. It's a lot nicer in there than it is out here.

They slow to a stop and BILL furtively looks around.

BILL

You . . . you live in there?

He sees the apartment building, its front door painted bright red.

DOMINO

Yes.

BILL

By yourself?

DOMINO

No. I have a room-mate but she's not home.
Hey, it's OK. Listen, no-one will bother us. It's
OK. Come on. Come on. . . .

DOMINO gently pulls him up the stoop to the front door.

47. INT. LOBBY – DOMINO APARTMENT
BUILDING – NIGHT

DOMINO leads BILL across the small, dingy lobby to a door on the ground floor. She unlocks the door and they enter.

48. INT. DOMINO APARTMENT – NIGHT

DOMINO comes in and BILL follows, looking around as he does. He notices a decorated Christmas tree in the hallway.

DOMINO

This is it.

BILL

A nice tree.

DOMINO laughs and leads him into a very messy kitchen.

DOMINO

Oh, sorry about the mess. Maid's day off.

BILL looks around then sits awkwardly on the edge of the bath tub.

BILL

It's a . . . it's a . . . cosy, cosy place.

DOMINO

It's OK.

There is an embarrassed silence as DOMINO takes off her hat and coat.

BILL

So, do you, do you suppose we should talk about money?

DOMINO

Yeah, I guess so. It depends on what you want to do. What *do* you wanna do?

BILL

Well, what do you recommend?

DOMINO

What do *I* recommend? Umm . . . well . . . I . . . I'd rather not put it into words. How about you just leave it up to me?

BILL

I'm in your hands.

DOMINO

OK . . . and how does a hundred and fifty sound?

> BILL

Sounds . . . wonderful.

> DOMINO

Don't worry, I don't keep track of the time.

49. INT. KITCHEN – BILL & ALICE'S APARTMENT –
NIGHT

*ALICE sits eating cookies and smoking a cigarette while
watching television. She is dressed in her blue silk dressing gown.*

50. INT. BEDROOM – DOMINO APARTMENT –
NIGHT

*DOMINO and BILL sit on the bed, faces close together.
Very slowly DOMINO leans forward and gently kisses
BILL on the lips. BILL, uncertain at first, responds a
little.*

> DOMINO

So, shall we?

*BILL's mobile phone rings. Hesitating for a moment, he
finally gets off the bed and walks across to the stereo
music centre and switches it off. He turns to DOMINO
and puts his finger to his lips so DOMINO will keep quiet.*

> BILL
> *(to Domino)*

Excuse me . . .

BILL faces the wall away from DOMINO as he takes the call.

> BILL

Hello?

51. INT. KITCHEN – BILL & ALICE'S APARTMENT –
NIGHT

ALICE is on the telephone.

> ALICE

Hi. . . .

52. INT. BEDROOM – DOMINO APARTMENT –
NIGHT

> BILL

Hi. Is everything all right?

53. INT. KITCHEN – BILL & ALICE'S APARTMENT –
NIGHT

ALICE

Yeah . . . I was, I was just wondering if you were
going to be much longer?

54. INT. BEDROOM – DOMINO APARTMENT –
NIGHT

BILL

Umm . . . listen, it's . . . it's a little difficult to
talk right now. It could be a while.

55. INT. KITCHEN – BILL & ALICE'S APARTMENT –
NIGHT

ALICE

Any idea how long?

56. INT. BEDROOM – DOMINO APARTMENT –
NIGHT

BILL

No, I don't really know. We're still waiting for
some relatives to arrive.

57. INT. KITCHEN – BILL & ALICE'S APARTMENT –
NIGHT

ALICE

Well, I'm . . . I'm gonna go to bed now.

58. INT. BEDROOM – DOMINO APARTMENT –
NIGHT

BILL

OK. Bye-bye.

ALICE *(o/s)*

Bye.

DOMINO is now leaning back on the bed.

DOMINO

Was that Mrs Dr Bill?

BILL, embarrassed, walks back towards the bed.

BILL

Yes . . . yes.

He sits down next to DOMINO again.

DOMINO

Do you have to go?

BILL

I have to go. I think I do.

                        DOMINO

Are you sure?

                          BILL

Yes, I'm afraid so. Ah, but listen, I want to pay
you anyway.

BILL takes his wallet out of his inside jacket pocket.

                          BILL

How much did you say it was? Hundred and
fifty?

                        DOMINO

Yeah, but you know what? You don't have to
bother about that.

                          BILL

No, it's all right.

                        DOMINO

No, really, you don't have to.

                          BILL

No, I want to.

                        DOMINO

Really?

BILL

Really.

BILL takes DOMINO's hand and presses the bills in it.

DOMINO

Well, thank you very much.

59. EXT. ANOTHER STREET – GREENWICH VILLAGE – NIGHT

BILL walks down a street and happens by the Café Sonata where NICK Nightingale mentioned he was playing. BILL stops and looks in the window where he sees a photograph of NICK sitting at the piano. BILL thinks for a moment then makes for the door, which is opened by a doorman.

BILL

Thank you.

60. INT. CAFÉ SONATA – NIGHT

BILL walks down the stairs of the club. We hear live music as BILL is greeted by the MAÎTRE D'.

MAÎTRE D'

Good evening, sir. Would you like a table or would you like to sit at the bar?

> BILL

I'd like a table.

> MAÎTRE D'

Please, follow me. Can I take your coat?

As BILL is taken to his table we see his friend, NICK, playing piano on stage with a jazz trio.

> BILL
> *(to Maître D')*

Thank you.

> MAÎTRE D'

Can I get you anything to drink?

> BILL

I'd like a beer.

> MAÎTRE D'

Certainly.

BILL watches the group as it finishes its final number. Then NICK quickly gets the band into the fast closing theme to cover his introductions to the musicians and his thanks to the audience.

> NICK

Hope you enjoyed the music tonight. We're

going to be here for the next two weeks. So, please, do stop by. I'm Nick Nightingale. Good night.

NICK leaves the stage and walks through the club.

VOICE FROM AUDIENCE
Nick, that was great!

NICK

Oh, thanks.

BILL

Nightingale!

NICK sees BILL and goes over to him.

NICK

Hey, Bill! You made it.

BILL

Yeah, listen, I'm sorry. I got here just as you were finishing your last set.

NICK

That's all right, the band sucked tonight anyway.

The MAÎTRE D' brings BILL his beer.

                    BILL
                (to Nick)
What are you drinking?

                    NICK
A vodka and tonic, please.

                    BILL
Thank you.

                    NICK
So what brings you out at this hour?

                    BILL
I have a patient in the neighbourhood.

                    NICK
Do you live in the Village?

                    BILL
No, we have an apartment on Central Park
West.

                    NICK
Are you married?

                    BILL
Nine years.

                    NICK
Do you have any kids?

                    BILL
Yes, we have a seven-year-old daughter. How
about you?

                    NICK
I've got a wife and four boys in Seattle.

                    BILL
You're a long way from home.

                    NICK
Yeah, well, you've gotta go where the work is.

The MAÎTRE D' brings NICK his drink.

                    NICK
Thank you.

They touch glasses then drink.

                    BILL
So, is this your band?

                    NICK
No, this is just a pick-up band.

                    BILL
Who do you normally play with?

                    NICK
Anybody, anywhere. As a matter of fact I got
another gig later tonight.

                    BILL
You're playing somewhere else tonight?

                    NICK
Mmm. . . . they only get started there around
two.

                    BILL
In the Village?

                    NICK
Believe it or not, I don't actually know the
address yet.

                    BILL
You don't?

                    NICK
No. It may sound ridiculous, but it's in a
different place every time and I only get it an
hour or so before.

                    BILL
Different place every time?

                    NICK
So far.

                    BILL
What's the big mystery?

NICK dangles his hands in front of BILL's face.

                    NICK
Hey, man! I just play the piano.

They start to giggle nervously.

                    BILL
Nick, I'm sorry. Is there something I'm missing
here?

                    NICK
I play blindfolded.

                    BILL
What?

                    NICK
Yeah, I play blindfolded.

> BILL

You're putting me on?

> NICK

No, it's the truth. And the last time, the
blindfold wasn't on so well . . . man . . . Bill, I
have seen one or two things in my life but
never, never anything like this . . . and never
such women.

> BILL

Well?

NICK's mobile phone rings. He takes it out of his pocket.

> NICK
> *(to Bill)*

Excuse me.
> *(speaking into phone)*

Hello? Yes, sir. Yes, sir. This is Nick. Uh-huh, I
know where that is.

*NICK takes a pen from his pocket and starts to write on
a paper napkin. He finds it difficult so BILL reaches
across and holds the napkin. NICK writes on it the word
"FIDELIO."*

> NICK

Uh-huh. . . . right. OK. Well, I'm on my way
right now. OK, sir. Thank you. Bye-bye.

                    BILL

What is this?

                    NICK

It's the name of a Beethoven opera, isn't it?

                    BILL

Nick. . . .

                    NICK

It's the password.

                    BILL

The password?

                    NICK

Yeah, like I'm . . . I'm really sorry to do this to
you, Bill. I mean, I . . . I gotta get going. I gotta
. . . I gotta go.

                    BILL

Nick, you know there is no way on earth that
you are going to leave here tonight without
taking me with you.

                    NICK

Come on, buddy, give me a break.

                    BILL

Nick, I'll tell you what. I've already got the
password. Just give me the address and I'll go
there by myself and there won't be any
connection between us whatsoever.

                    NICK

Listen, let's just say for one second that I was
prepared to do that. You couldn't get in anyway
in those clothes.

                    BILL

Why not?

                    NICK

Because everyone is always costumed and
masked, and where the hell are you gonna get a
costume at this hour of the morning?

61. EXT. ANOTHER STREET – GREENWICH
VILLAGE – NIGHT

*A taxi turns the corner and pulls up outside a costume
shop named RAINBOW FASHIONS. BILL gets out of the
cab and pays the driver.*

                    BILL
Thanks. Keep the change.

BILL walks up the stoop and rings the bell. A voice responds through the intercom with a heavy Slavic accent. This is MILICH.

MILICH *(o/s)*
Yes? Who is it?

BILL
Peter, this is Bill Harford. I apologize for disturbing you at this late hour but I need your help.

MILICH *(o/s)*
Who is it that you want?

BILL
Oh! I . . . I'm very sorry, I'm looking for Peter Grenning, the owner of Rainbow Fashions.

MILICH *(o/s)*
What's your name?

BILL
My name is Bill Harford. I'm Mr Grenning's doctor.

MILICH *(o/s)*
You are Grenning's doctor?

>   BILL
> Yes.

>   MILICH *(o/s)*
> OK. Just a moment.

BILL looks through the plate glass and sees a door open inside. From it a man appears and walks towards BILL. The man is middle-aged, has a beard and long hair and wears a dressing gown. This is MILICH.

62. INT. HALLWAY – RAINBOW FASHIONS – NIGHT

MILICH talks to BILL who stands on the steps outside the locked door.

>   MILICH
> You are looking for Peter Grenning?

>   BILL
> Yes, I am.

>   MILICH
> He moved to Chicago – over a year ago.

>   BILL
> He moved to Chicago? Oh, I wasn't aware of that. Are you the present owner of Rainbow Fashions?

MILICH

Yes, I am.

BILL

Well, first of all, please let me apologize once
again for disturbing you at this hour, Mr
umm? . . .

MILICH

Milich.

BILL

Mr Milich. Just to let you know that I really am
Dr Harford, this is my New York State Medical
Board Card.
(holds wallet to glass)

MILICH

OK, so you are Dr Harford and if I see Peter I
tell him you were looking for him.

BILL

Oh, no, no! Wait, please, please. Listen, the
reason that I came here tonight was umm . . .
basically the reason is, is that I need a costume.
And I'd be happy to pay you a hundred dollars
over the rental price for the inconvenience.

MILICH

A hundred dollars?

> BILL

Yes.

> MILICH

I don't think so.

> BILL

Well, erh, OK. How about two hundred dollars?

> MILICH

Two hundred dollars over the rental price?

> BILL

Yes.

> MILICH

OK.

63. INT. MAIN AREA – RAINBOW FASHIONS – NIGHT

MILICH opens the door, lets BILL in, then closes it behind them.

> MILICH

Come in.

MILICH disables the burglar alarm system.

MILICH

Can't be too careful these days, hmm.
                    (indicates)
Please.

MILICH leads BILL through the shop to a counter. He switches on a lamp.

MILICH

Is it any special costume you are looking for?

BILL

Yes, umm . . . I need a tux, a cloak with a hood, and a mask.

MILICH

A cloak with a hood and a mask?

BILL

Yes.

MILICH

OK. I think we find something for you. Follow me, please.

MILICH leads BILL into another room of the shop.

64. INT. INNER ROOM – RAINBOW FASHIONS – NIGHT

MILICH
(pointing to mannequins)
Looks like alive, huh?

BILL
Yes, it's wonderful.

MILICH
Come. So, what colour cloak?

BILL
Umm. . . .

MILICH
Black, brown, red?

BILL
Black.

MILICH
Are you sure the good doctor wouldn't like
something more colourful?

BILL
I don't think so.

MILICH
Clowns? Officers? Pirates?

BILL

No, just the tux, the black cloak. . . .

MILICH

With a hood and the mask.

BILL

Yes.

MILICH

OK. May I take your coat?

BILL

Yes.

BILL takes his coat and gives it to MILICH.

MILICH

You are medicine doctor, yes?

BILL

Yes, I am.

MILICH

Oh, look, doctor. I have some problem with my hair, you know?

BILL

Your hair?

MILICH

It's starting to fall down, too fast. I lost in two weeks a lot of hair, mostly here. Look at this, here.

MILICH bends over to show his balding patch. BILL quickly examines it.

BILL

Oh, yes.

MILICH

You see?

BILL

Yes.

MILICH

And?

BILL

I'm afraid this really isn't my field.

MILICH

What, you can't help me?

BILL

No, you should see a trichologist – it's a hair

specialist . . . Mr Milich. I've obviously left
things a bit late tonight, so if you don't
mind. . . .

MILICH

OK, OK. I'm in hurry too, doctor. To get back to
bed.

BILL

I understand.

*MILICH casts BILL's overcoat aside and goes to a rail of
hooded cloaks.*

MILICH

So, black cloak?

Suddenly, MILICH stops and turns to BILL.

MILICH

Did you hear something? What is it?

*MILICH walks towards a room behind a glass wall at
the back of the shop. He peers through the glass into the
darkness to try to see where the noise came from.*

MILICH

What is it?

MILICH goes into the room through a door and switches on a light. He looks down to a low table laden with the remains of take-away meals. MILICH picks up a girl's slip and suddenly hears a sound behind him. He pulls aside a robe hanging on the wall to reveal a JAPANESE MAN in underpants and fright wig who sneezes. MIL-ICH angrily grabs the wig and explodes in anger.

MILICH

What is this? What on earth is going on here?

JAPANESE MAN 1
(very frightened)
Oh, Milich! I can explain everything.

MILICH notices something behind the sofa. He attacks it with the wig in his hand and up jumps a young girl dressed only in a bra and panties. This is MILICH's DAUGHTER.

MILICH
(to Daughter)
You! What are you doing here? I'll kill you! I promise I'll kill you!

Another JAPANESE MAN in a wig and covering his "modesty" with a cloth pops up from behind the sofa. MILICH grabs his wig and attacks him with it.

MILICH

And you, have you no sense of decency!?
Gentlemen, have you no sense of decency!?

The DAUGHTER grabs a shawl to cover herself.

JAPANESE MAN 1

Milich, are you crazy? We were invited here by
the young lady.

MILICH

Young lady? This is my daughter! Couldn't you
see she's a child? You will have to explain to
police.

JAPANESE MAN 1

To the police?

*MILICH makes for his DAUGHTER but she's off around
the sofa. MILICH tries to catch her but she evades him.
She runs into the shop and stands behind BILL who cannot understand what's going on.*

MILICH
(to Daughter)
You little whore! I'll kill you for this! I promise,
I'll kill you! . . . I'll kill you!
(to Bill)
Hold on to that girl for me, please.

BILL looks at the DAUGHTER as she smiles up at him.

JAPANESE MAN 1 *(o/s)*
Milich, this is preposterous. The young lady
invited us here.

*MILICH angrily throws some clothing at the two cower-
ing JAPANESE MEN.*

MILICH
Couldn't you see? She's . . . deranged!
(then to Bill)
Doctor, I'm sorry to keep you waiting.
(to Japanese)
Gentlemen, this is now police matter. You will
please stay here until I return.

*MILICH leaves the room and locks the door behind him,
trapping the men inside.*

JAPANESE MAN 1
Milich, what are you doing? Let us out of here.

MILICH
I'm afraid that's out of the question.
(to Bill)
Doctor, sorry, what colour did you say?

BILL
Umm. . . .

MILICH

Black?

BILL

Black.

MILICH
(to Japanese men)
Gentlemen, please . . . have the goodness to be
quiet for the moment. Couldn't you see I try to
serve my customer?
(to Bill)
Sorry.
(to Daughter)
And you, little whore, go to bed at once, you
depraved creature! I'll deal with you as soon as
I serve this gentlemen.

DAUGHTER
(whispers into Bill's ear)
You should have a cloak lined with ermine.

*The DAUGHTER slowly leaves the room, giving BILL a
suggestive look as she goes. BILL looks at her perplexed.*

65. EXT. TAXI CAB – BROOKLYN BRIDGE – NIGHT

A taxi speeds over the bridge.

66. INT. TAXI CAB – NIGHT

BILL sits in the cab alone with his churning thoughts.

67. INT. ROOM – CAPE COD – DAY

BILL's relentless fantasy returns as he imagines the NAVAL OFFICER and his wife making love.

68. INT. TAXI CAB – NIGHT

BILL closes his eyes as if to shut out the thought of his wife with another man.

69. INT. TAXI CAB – POV BILL – NIGHT

BILL's view from the cab as it swings off the bridge and onto a link road which will take it through the suburbs and out to the country.

70. EXT. TAXI CAB – SUBURBAN ROAD – NIGHT

The taxi drives through the suburbs. Festive illuminations strung across the road proclaim "HAPPY HOLIDAY."

71. EXT. TAXI CAB – COUNTRY ROAD – NIGHT

The cab proceeds down a tree-lined country road.

72. INT. TAXI CAB – NIGHT

BILL looks out to see where he is.

73. INT. TAXI CAB – POV BILL – NIGHT

BILL's POV: the entry gates of a large country house can be seen through the trees to the right. Two men in dark coats are waiting in front of them. A sign shows the name of the house as "Somerton." The two men watch the cab closely.

74. EXT. ENTRY GATES – NIGHT

The taxi slows to a halt.

75. INT. TAXI CAB – NIGHT

The TAXI DRIVER switches on his light and BILL opens his wallet.

> CAB DRIVER
> OK. That's seventy-four fifty.

> BILL
> Seventy-four fifty, all right. There's eighty. I
> promised you fifty bucks over the meter, right?
> I'll make that a hundred . . . if you wait for me.

BILL holds up a $100 bill and tears it in half.

                    BILL

So, let the meter run. I'll give you the other half,
plus the meter, when I get back. OK?

                 CAB DRIVER

How long you gonna be?

                    BILL

I dunno, maybe an hour or more, but maybe
only ten minutes. I'll leave my stuff here in the
back. OK?

                 CAB DRIVER

OK.

*The TAXI DRIVER takes one half of the $100 note and
BILL gets out of the cab.*

76. EXT. ENTRY GATES – NIGHT

*BILL closes the cab door and slowly walks towards the
two GATEMEN.*

                 GATEMAN 1

Good evening, sir.

                    BILL

Good evening.

GATEMAN 1

Can we be of any help?

BILL

Well, I suppose you'd like the password?

GATEMAN 1

If you like, sir.

BILL

Fidelio.

GATEMAN 1

Thank you, sir. We'll run you up to the house.

The GATEMAN gestures to a vehicle on the other side of the gates.

77. EXT. "SOMERTON" – NIGHT

A vast country house set amidst its own grounds. Limousines of all descriptions are lined up each side of the driveway. The vehicle ferrying BILL drives up and stops. BILL steps out and then walks up to the front door which is opened for him. BILL enters the house.

78. INT. PILLARED HALLWAY – "SOMERTON" – NIGHT

BILL walks in and is approached by a MASKED BUT-LER. The sound of strange music can be heard in the background.

                    MASKED BUTLER

Good evening, sir.

                         BILL

Good evening.

                    MASKED BUTLER

Password, sir.

                         BILL

Fidelio.

                        BUTLER

Thank you, sir.

*The MASKED BUTLER takes BILL's coat. Underneath
BILL is wearing a hooded cloak. BILL then puts his mask
on and pulls the hood over his head as he walks towards
another door which is opened for him by a MASKED
MAN. BILL enters.*

79. INT. ANTE-ROOM/MARBLE HALL –
"SOMERTON" – NIGHT

*BILL comes in through the door and walks slowly across
the ante-room. A STEWARD, also masked, elegantly gestures him through heavy velvet drapes into a vast hall –
its walls, ceilings, balconies and columns all finely
carved in white marble. The hall is crowded with people*

dressed similarly to BILL: black hooded cloaks and full-faced Venetian Carnival-style masks of every conceivable design and colour.

BILL sees a brightly lit circle of kneeling figures. In the centre is a figure wearing a red cloak who is conducting a strange ritual (this is RED CLOAK). He is waving an incense burner in one hand while holding a staff in the other.

At the far end of the hall BILL sees NICK heavily blindfolded and dressed in a white tuxedo. NICK is sitting at an array of keyboards producing eerie music that resonates through the hall and up to the marble balconies and galleries where gather cloaked and masked spectators.

RED CLOAK now walks slowly around the circle of figures and then moves to the centre. He bows deeply and the kneeling figures prostrate themselves before him. From a column furthest away from the spectacle BILL watches as RED CLOAK bangs his staff on the red carpet, a command that returns the figures to their kneeling positions. Then he moves slowly around the circle swinging the incense burner before moving back to the centre and banging the staff again which causes the figures to rise to their feet.

RED CLOAK bangs the staff on the carpet a further time: the figures unclasp the hooks of their cloaks and let them fall off their shoulders to the floor. The figures are now revealed to be beautiful young women, naked except for their masks and G-strings.

As RED CLOAK turns on the spot one of the women leans to her right to lightly embrace the woman next to her. She places a kiss on her lips. The kissed woman now leans to her right and repeats the act with the next woman, the kiss now being "passed" around the circle.

While BILL tries to fathom what is happening two figures on a balcony opposite seem to be taking a more than passing interest in him. They continue staring at BILL until he slowly becomes aware of them. One of the figures wears a tricorn mask while the other hides behind an androgynous mask. There is a sinister air to both of them. The man in the tricorn mask bows to BILL, seemingly in recognition. BILL, uncertain at first, returns the bow. Then his attention is drawn back to the women in the circle.

RED CLOAK, with a rap of his staff on the floor, commands a woman to her feet. The woman bows to RED CLOAK who then bestows a "blessing" upon her. She then leaves the circle and approaches a man in the surrounding crowd. She leans forward to "kiss" the man, their masked lips touching, before leading him off out of the hall.

BILL watches as the procedure is repeated with the "blessed" women apparently choosing men at random from the spectators.

RED CLOAK has now reached a woman in the circle who wears a mask more alluring than the others, a beautiful design with black feathered plumes arising above her head (this is MYSTERIOUS WOMAN). After receiving the "blessing" the MYSTERIOUS WOMAN turns and walks straight to BILL.

She gently places her hand on his shoulder as she leans forward to "kiss" him. Then she leads BILL by the hand out of the hall.

80. INT. RED CARPETED CORRIDOR –
"SOMERTON" – NIGHT

The MYSTERIOUS WOMAN leads BILL down a red car-
peted corridor which, like the hall, has walls of carved
marble. On these walls are large mirrors which reflect
the procession of almost-naked women leading the
masked men away.

MYSTERIOUS WOMAN
(unexpectedly)

I'm not sure what you think you're doing, but
you don't belong here.

BILL

I'm sorry, but I think you've mistaken me for
someone else.

MYSTERIOUS WOMAN

Please don't be foolish. You must go now.

BILL

Who are you?

MYSTERIOUS WOMAN

It doesn't matter who I am. You're in great
danger. And you must get away while there is
still a chance.

An OMINOUS MAN in a large, almost over-sized mask, suddenly appears and takes the MYSTERIOUS WOMAN's arm

OMINOUS MAN
(to Bill)
Would you be so good as to excuse us for a moment?

The OMINOUS MAN leads the MYSTERIOUS WOMAN away up a marble staircase. She looks back at BILL who is left wondering what is going on in the house.

81. INT. BALCONIED HALLWAY – "SOMERTON" – NIGHT

BILL follows a couple into a large hall that also has walls of carved marble. There are many doors and archways leading off.

A beautiful naked young woman is astride a man on his back. They are fucking and oblivious to the spectators crowded all around them.

At the end of the room a naked man eases a woman in an elegant dress on to a polished table. He begins fucking her, unaware of BILL who passes closely by.

82. INT. LONG TABLE ROOM – "SOMERTON" – NIGHT

BILL enters the room. On a long table two naked women in a "sixty-nine" position simulate mutual cunnilingus.

Three other women sit on stools upon the table slowly and sensuously caressing each other's bodies. Gathered around the table are masked voyeurs enjoying the spectacle.

BILL continues through the house.

83. INT. ANTE-ROOM/LIBRARY – "SOMERTON" – NIGHT

BILL enters the ante-room. The focus of the crowd's attention is a naked woman, her hands held down by a masked woman in a red dress, who is being fucked from behind by a naked man.

BILL walks through and into a sumptuous library with oak paneled walls and bookcases full of leather bound volumes.

A roaring fire illuminates the bizarre scene of a masked man in formal evening dress on his hands and knees while on his back is a naked woman being fucked by another man in a Pan-like mask.

BILL joins the other onlookers. Then the man in the tricorn mask enters the room accompanied by a naked YOUNG WOMAN. They stop and upon a signal from the man the YOUNG WOMAN walks up to BILL and stands next to him.

YOUNG WOMAN
Have you been enjoying yourself?

BILL
I've had a very interesting look around.

                    YOUNG WOMAN
Do you want to go somewhere a little more
private?

                        BILL
Private? That might be a good idea.

*Suddenly, the MYSTERIOUS WOMAN in the beautiful
feathered mask walks up to BILL and interrupts the conversation.*

                MYSTERIOUS WOMAN
Oh, there you are! I've been looking all over for
you. Where did you go?
                    (to Girl)
May I borrow him for just a few minutes? I
promise to bring him right back.

*The MYSTERIOUS WOMAN takes BILL by the hand and
leads him out of the library.*

84. INT. SMALL HALL – "SOMERTON" – NIGHT

*The MYSTERIOUS WOMAN looks around her to make
sure no one is about and then takes BILL across the hall.*

                MYSTERIOUS WOMAN
I don't think you realize the danger you're in
now. You can't fool them for much longer.
You've got to get away before it's too late.

                    BILL

Why are you telling me this?

                MYSTERIOUS WOMAN

It doesn't matter.

                    BILL

Who are you?

                MYSTERIOUS WOMAN

You don't want to know, but you must go now.

                    BILL

Will you come with me?

                MYSTERIOUS WOMAN

That's impossible.

                    BILL

Why?

                MYSTERIOUS WOMAN

Because it would cost me my life and possibly
yours.

                    BILL

Let me see your face.

BILL attempts to remove her mask but she holds tight.

> MYSTERIOUS WOMAN

No!

She finally pushes his hands away and then leaves quickly.

> MYSTERIOUS WOMAN

Go!

BILL looks towards her but before he can do anything a TALL BUTLER arrives. He too is masked.

> TALL BUTLER

Excuse me, sir. Are you the gentleman with the taxi waiting for you?

> BILL

Yes.

> TALL BUTLER

Your driver's at the front door and would urgently like a word with you.

He gestures BILL to follow him and they leave the room.

85. INT. LARGE PALM-LINED HALL –
"SOMERTON" – NIGHT

Couples dance, some naked, some in evening dress, as NICK Nightingale, still blindfolded, is led through the room and away down a corridor.

86. INT. RED CARPETED CORRIDOR –
"SOMERTON" – NIGHT

The TALL BUTLER escorts BILL down the same corridor along which the MYSTERIOUS WOMAN had earlier led BILL. As they reach the door of the white marble hall where BILL had witnessed the opening ritual, they stop. There, in the middle of the red carpet, sits RED CLOAK on a throne with acolytes in purple robes standing either side of him. They are surrounded by a circle of many people in black cloaks and masks.

RED CLOAK beckons BILL to him.

RED CLOAK
Please come forward.

As BILL enters the gap in the circle, the men in black cloaks close rank, cutting off any way of escape.

RED CLOAK
May I have the password, please?

BILL
Fidelio.

RED CLOAK
That's right, sir. That is the password for admittance . . . but may I ask what is the password for the house?

                    BILL
The password for the house?

                  RED CLOAK
Yes.

                    BILL
I'm sorry I . . . I . . . I seem to have forgotten it.

                  RED CLOAK
That's unfortunate, because here it doesn't
matter whether you have forgotten it or if you
never knew it. You will kindly remove your
mask.
                  (pause)
Now get undressed.

                    BILL
Get undressed?

                  RED CLOAK
Remove your clothes.

                    BILL
Gentlemen, please. . . .

                  RED CLOAK
Remove your clothes, or would you like us to
do it for you?

Suddenly, there is a shout from the balcony behind BILL.

MYSTERIOUS WOMAN
Stop! Let him go. Take me, I am ready to redeem
him.

*There is a gasp of surprise from the crowd. RED CLOAK
gets to his feet.*

RED CLOAK
You are ready to redeem him?

MYSTERIOUS WOMAN
Yes.

Another gasp of surprise from the crowd.

RED CLOAK
Are you sure you understand what you are
taking upon yourself in doing this?

MYSTERIOUS WOMAN
Yes.

RED CLOAK
(severely to Bill)
Very well. You are free, but I warn you if you
make any further inquires or if you say a single
word to anyone about what you have seen,
there will be the most dire consequences for
you and your family. Do you understand?

BILL slowly nods his understanding and looks up to the MYSTERIOUS WOMAN on the balcony. The BIRD MASK MAN then takes her away.

>   BILL
> What . . . what is going to happen to that
> woman?

>   RED CLOAK
> No one can change her fate now. When a
> promise has been made here, there is no turning
> back. Go!

87. INT. BILL & ALICE'S APARTMENT – NIGHT

The front door of the apartment opens and BILL comes in carrying a bag with his costume. He quietly shuts and locks the front door. He walks down the hallway and looks in at HELENA's room. She lies fast asleep. BILL turns away and walks on down through the living room, taking off his coat as he does, and into his study. He unlocks a cupboard and hides the bag with his costume there.

88. INT. BEDROOM – BILL & ALICE'S APARTMENT – NIGHT

BILL walks into the bedroom to find ALICE asleep but murmuring in a dream. He sits on the side of the bed, and ALICE's noises turn to laughing. As the laugh be-

comes almost hysterical BILL gently touches her. She awakes with a "start" and is a little distressed.

BILL

Alice . . . Alice . . . OK. It's OK. I'm sorry, I'm sorry I woke you up but I thought you were having a nightmare.

BILL starts to take off his shoes as ALICE tries to calm down.

ALICE

Oh, God . . . I just had such a horrible dream. What time is it?

BILL

Er, a little after four.

ALICE

Did you just get home?

BILL

Yes, it took longer . . . longer than I thought.

ALICE

You must be exhausted. Come on, lie down, lie down.

ALICE, still slightly upset, reaches out to him and pulls BILL down next to her.

                    BILL
What were you dreaming?

                    ALICE
It's just a . . . just these weird things.

                    BILL
What was it?

                    ALICE
Oh . . . so weird.

                    BILL
Tell me.

ALICE sits up, trying to recapture her dream.

                    ALICE
We . . . we were . . . we were in a deserted city
and . . . and our clothes were gone. We were
naked, and . . . and I was terrified, and I . . . I
felt ashamed. Oh, God! And . . . and I was angry
because I felt it was your fault. You . . . you
rushed away to try and find our clothes for us.
As soon as you were gone it was completely
different. I . . . I felt wonderful. Then I was
lying in a . . . in a beautiful garden, stretched
out naked in the sunlight, and a man walked
out of the woods, he was . . . he was the man

from the hotel, the one I told you about . . . the
naval officer. He . . . he stared at me and then
he just laughed . . . he just laughed at me.

ALICE lies down again, burying her face in her pillow.
BILL sits up and looks at her crying into the pillow.

BILL

That's not the end, is it?

ALICE

No.

BILL

Why don't you tell me the rest of it?

ALICE

It's . . . it's too awful.

BILL

It's only a dream.

ALICE gets close to BILL and envelopes him in her arms
while summoning the courage to continue the story.

ALICE

He . . . he was kissing me, and then . . . then we
were making love. Then there were all these
other people around us . . . hundreds of them,

everywhere. Everyone was fucking, and then I
. . . I was fucking other men, so many . . . I don't
know how many I was with. And I knew you
could see me in the arms of all these men, just
fucking all these men, and I . . . I wanted to
make fun of you, to laugh in your face. And so I
laughed as loud as I could. And that must have
been when you woke me up.

*She weeps and caresses BILL who is perplexed and sits
not knowing what to feel about what she has told him.*

89. EXT. STREET – NEW YORK – MORNING

The following morning. A street full of traffic. Crowds.

90. EXT. CAFÉ SONATA – DAY

*A taxi pulls up and BILL gets out. He is carrying the bag
with his costume from the night before. He walks up to
the Café Sonata and sees the entrance grill closed and
locked.*

                         BILL
Shit. . . .

*He wonders what to do. He looks around and sees that
Gillespie's Coffee Shop next door is open. He goes inside.*

91. INT. GILLESPIE'S COFFEE SHOP – DAY

BILL walks in and finds a seat at the counter. An attractive WAITRESS behind the counter greets him.

> WAITRESS
>
> Hi!

> BILL
>
> Hi. I'll just have a cup of coffee, please.

She pours BILL a cup.

> WAITRESS
>
> Anything else?

> BILL
>
> No, thank you.

The WAITRESS writes a check and lays it in front of him.

> BILL
>
> Excuse me, would you happen to know when they get in next door at the Sonata Café?

> WAITRESS
>
> I think there's usually someone in the office round two or three.

BILL

Round two or three. Umm . . . I, erh . . . I don't
suppose, by any chance, you know Nick
Nightingale? He's playing piano over there right
now?

WAITRESS

Nick Nightingale? Sure, he comes in here.

BILL

Look . . . look maybe you can help me, because
it's very important that I get in touch with him
this morning. Do you know where he's staying?

WAITRESS

Well . . . I, I don't know whether he would want
me to give out his address.

BILL

It's OK, I'm a doctor. I'm . . . I'm actually a very
old friend of his.

BILL shows her his State Medical Board card.

WAITRESS

Well, doctor, umm . . . he'll be playing there
tonight. Can it wait until then?

BILL

Listen, to be perfectly honest, erh . . . it's a

medical matter, some tests. And I know he'll
wanna know about them as soon as possible.

92. EXT. ANOTHER STREET – NEW YORK – DAY

*The morning traffic is in full flow. The streets crowded
with pedestrians. BILL, carrying his bag, walks up the
street and comes to the Hotel Jason. He goes in.*

93. INT. LOBBY – HOTEL JASON – DAY

*It's a clean, respectable, moderately priced establish-
ment. BILL walks up to the reception desk and calls to
the gay CLERK who is putting a letter in a guest's
pigeon-hole.*

> BILL

Excuse me.

> CLERK

Hi! How can I help you?

> BILL

Can you please ring Mr. Nightingale's room for
me? Nick Nightingale.

> CLERK

I'm sorry, sir. Mr. Nightingale has already
checked out.

                       BILL

He checked out?

                       CLERK

Yes.

                       BILL

Er . . . did he leave a forwarding address?

                       CLERK

No, I'm afraid not, no.

                       BILL

When did he check out?

                       CLERK

Umm . . . about five o'clock this morning.

                       BILL

Five o'clock this morning?

                       CLERK

Yes.

                       BILL

It's a pretty early check out, isn't it?

CLERK

It is a little on the early side, yeah.

BILL

Look . . . did you notice anything, I dunno,
unusual about him when he left?

CLERK

Unusual? Hey! You're not Five O, are you?

BILL

No, I'm an old friend of his.

CLERK

Really?

BILL

I'm a doctor.

CLERK

Oh.

*BILL shows him his State Medical Board Card. The
CLERK starts getting very friendly.*

CLERK

Well, umm . . . *Bill*?

BILL

Sure.

CLERK

It's funny you should ask that question, Bill,
because actually there was something a little
strange about the way Mr. Nightingale left, yes.

BILL

Really, what? What was that?

CLERK

Well . . . he came in this morning about four-
thirty a.m. with two men. Big guys. I mean,
they were very well dressed and very well
spoken but they weren't the kind of people
you'd like to fool around with . . . if you know
what I mean. Anyway, I noticed Mr.
Nightingale had a bruise on his cheek and umm
. . . to be perfectly honest, I also thought he
looked a little scared.

BILL

Scared?

CLERK

Yes, yes. He . . . he said he wanted to check out
and then he went upstairs to his room with one
of the men and the other guy stayed down in

the lobby and settled his bill. And then, when
they came back down, Mr. Nightingale tried to
pass me an envelope but they saw it and and
took it away and said that any mail or messages
for him would be collected by someone properly
authorized to do so. And then they just took him
off in a car.

BILL
Do you have any idea where they went?

CLERK
No, not a clue.

BILL
Um . . . well, anyway . . . I certainly . . . I
certainly appreciate your help.

CLERK
Oh! Anytime, Bill. Bye!

BILL leaves the Hotel Jason.

94. EXT. STREET – GREENWICH VILLAGE – DAY

*A taxi pulls up outside RAINBOW FASHIONS where BILL
had hired the costume the night before. BILL gets out the
cab with his bag and ascends the stoop.*

95. INT. RAINBOW FASHIONS – DAY

BILL walks to the counter and puts the bag on it.

MILICH

Oh, the good doctor.

BILL

Mr Milich.

MILICH

Was your outfit the success?

BILL

Yes, it was. Thank you.

MILICH starts to take the costume out of the bag.

MILICH

Good, good.
                    (pause)
Tuxedo, cloak, shoes, erh . . . I think you forgot
the mask.

BILL

It's not there?

BILL, troubled, picks through the clothes on the counter.

MILICH

No, no, no. Maybe you left it at the party?

BILL

Er . . . I don't think so. I must have lost it. Can you just put it on the bill, please?

MILICH

Sure.

MILICH opens the till and takes out the receipt from the night before.

MILICH

Here we are. That was one hundred fifty for the rental, two hundred you said for my trouble, twenty five for the mask – sorry. That's . . . three hundred and seventy-five.

Then the door at the end of the shop opens and the DAUGHTER appears who BILL saw with the JAPANESE MEN. She has only her bra and panties on with a flimsy kimono.

MILICH

(to Daughter)

Yes, dear . . . come, come.

The DAUGHTER walks to the counter and stands next to MILICH.

                    MILICH
Would you like to say hello to Dr Harford?

                    DAUGHTER
                    (to Bill)
Hello!

She offers her hand to BILL and they shake.

                    BILL
Hello.

Then the JAPANESE MEN appear through the door, both smartly dressed. They hesitate on seeing BILL and then they slowly walk up to MILICH and his DAUGHTER.

                    JAPANESE MAN 1
Thank you, Mr Milich. I'll call you soon.
Bye-bye.

They take their leave, one of them blowing a kiss to the DAUGHTER.

                    MILICH
Goodbye, gentlemen. Merry Christmas and
happy new year!
                    (pause)
Well, Dr Harford, there is your receipt. I'm
tearing up your deposits, and thanks for the
business.

While MILICH does this BILL looks at the DAUGHTER who returns a knowing look. BILL is shocked by what he has seen.

BILL

Mr Milich, last night . . . you were going to call the police.

MILICH

Well . . . things change. We have come to another arrangement. And, by the way, if the good doctor himself should ever want anything again – *anything* at all. . . .

MILICH puts his arm around his DAUGHTER's shoulders. BILL sees the fragile, china doll-like face of the girl.

MILICH
(suggestively)
It needn't be a costume. . . .

BILL is left speechless at this invitation.

96. EXT. AVENUE – NEW YORK – DAY

A busy avenue with office blocks in mid-town Manhattan.

97. INT. PRIVATE OFFICE – BILL'S SURGERY – DAY

BILL, in his white doctor's coat, sits deep in thought.

98. INT. ROOM – CAPE COD – DAY

BILL continues to brood over the fantasy of ALICE making love with the NAVAL OFFICER.

99. INT. PRIVATE OFFICE – BILL'S SURGERY – DAY

BILL, still wrapped up in his thoughts, is interrupted by a knock at the door.

                    BILL
Come in.

LISA comes in with a "take-away" food bag and coffee.

                    LISA
Tuna salad and black coffee.

                    BILL
Thanks. Listen, how's my afternoon looking?

                    LISA
I think it's just Mrs Akerly at two-thirty and
Mrs Kominski at four.

                    BILL
Well, look, something's come up and I'm not
going to be able to see them. Please ask Dr
Miller if he can fit them in, otherwise just
apologize and make new appointments.

                    LISA

Sure.

                    BILL

And please, call the garage and have them get
my car out in half an hour.

                    LISA

No problem.

                    BILL

OK?

                    LISA

Sure.

100. EXT. RANGE ROVER – BROOKLYN BRIDGE –
DAY

BILL's Range Rover speeds over the bridge.

101. INT. RANGE ROVER – DAY

BILL continues driving over the bridge.

102. EXT. RANGE ROVER – FREEWAY – DAY

BILL's Range Rover on its way through the suburbs.

103. EXT. COUNTRY ROAD – DAY

BILL's Range Rover slows down on a road lined with fir trees. It turns into the gateway of "Somerton," the house where the masked ball had been held the night before, and comes to a halt to the fore of the gates. Nobody is about.

BILL gets out of the Range Rover and slowly walks to the closed gates. He looks up and sees a surveillance camera tracking him. He is wondering what to do when he sees a limousine coming down the driveway towards him. It comes to a stop the other side of the gates.

An ELDERLY MAN, smartly dressed, gets out of the car and walks up to the gates while keeping a steady eye on BILL. He takes a letter from his inside pocket and pushes it through the gate.

BILL approaches the ELDERLY MAN and takes the letter. Without saying a word, the man turns, goes back to the car and is driven away.

BILL looks at the envelope and sees "DR. WILLIAM HARFORD" typed on it. He opens it and takes out a sheet of paper. Written on it is a warning to him:

> Give up your inquiries which are completely useless, and consider these words a second warning. We hope, for your own good, that this will be sufficient.

BILL thinks long and hard about this warning and what it implies. He turns away from the gates to go back to his car.

104. EXT. BILL & ALICE'S APARTMENT – NIGHT

Night time traffic. Illuminations. People walking about.

105. INT. BILL & ALICE'S APARTMENT – NIGHT

BILL comes in through the front door and closes it. He is wearing an overcoat and carrying a case. He walks down the corridor.

> ALICE *(o/s)*

Hi!

> HELENA *(o/s)*

Hi, daddy!

> BILL
> *(walking)*

Hi! Any calls for me?

BILL takes his coat off and drops it over a chair in the hallway. He continues into the dining room where he sees ALICE sitting with HELENA doing some homework. ALICE seems pleased to see him. BILL kisses ALICE on the head and strokes HELENA's hair.

> ALICE *(o/s)*

Dr Sanders and, erh . . . Mrs Shapiro.

> HELENA

Hi, daddy!

> BILL

Hey. . . .

HELENA proudly shows him her schoolbook.

                         HELENA
Look, I got all these right.

                          BILL
You got all those right?

                         HELENA
Yeah.

                          BILL
Every single one of them?

                         HELENA
Ah-hah. . . .

                          BILL
That's good.

                         ALICE
You hungry?

                          BILL
Er . . . sort of.

                         ALICE
Want to eat at seven?

BILL

Ooh! Seven. Listen, can we make that a little
earlier because I have some appointments at
the office?

ALICE

You have to go out again, tonight?

BILL

Mmm, afraid so.

HELENA

Daddy, am I gonna get a puppy for Christmas?

BILL
(kissing Helena)
Well, we'll . . . we'll see about that OK?

*BILL walks into the kitchen, opens the fridge and takes
out a drink.*

HELENA

He could be a watchdog?

BILL

We'll see.

ALICE

Come on, baby, let's finish this off. All right, we

have Joe and Joe has two dollars fifty, Mike has
one dollar and seventy-five cents. Joe has how
much more money than Mike?

HELENA

One hundred and seventy-five.

ALICE

So, is it going to be a subtraction or addition?

HELENA

Hmmm . . . how much more means that it
would be an subtraction, wouldn't it?

ALICE

Yeah, so you are going to be taking, right. . . .

*As ALICE helps HELENA with her homework BILL
watches from the kitchen as ALICE's words from the
night before come back to haunt him:*

ALICE *(v/o)*

And there were all these other people.
Hundreds of them everywhere, and everyone
was fucking. And then I . . . I was fucking other
men, so many, I . . . I don't know how many I
was with.

While BILL can hear her voice in his head ALICE gives him a look full of love and affection. BILL responds with a forced smile.

106. INT. RECEPTION AREA – BILL'S SURGERY – NIGHT

The Christmas lights illuminate the area. At the end of the reception we see a door ajar and light coming through it.

107. INT. PRIVATE OFFICE – BILL'S SURGERY – NIGHT

BILL sits staring at the telephone.

108. INT. ROOM – CAPE COD – DAY

The thought of ALICE making love with the NAVAL OFFI-CER invades BILL's mind again.

109. INT. PRIVATE OFFICE – BILL'S SURGERY – NIGHT

BILL, still staring at his phone, decides to act. He picks up the receiver and punches in a number.

110. INT. HALLWAY – NATHANSON APARTMENT – NIGHT

The phone rings in the hallway. CARL walks down the corridor and picks up the receiver.

CARL

Hello? Hello? Hello?

111. INT. PRIVATE OFFICE – BILL'S SURGERY – NIGHT

BILL is disappointed at hearing CARL's voice. He had been expecting MARION to answer.

112. INT. HALLWAY – NATHANSON APARTMENT – NIGHT

CARL is still trying to get a response from the telephone.

113. INT. PRIVATE OFFICE – BILL'S SURGERY – NIGHT

BILL thinks for a moment, then puts the phone down. He is clearly troubled.

114. EXT. DOMINO APARTMENT BUILDING – NIGHT

A taxi pulls up at the curbside outside DOMINO's apartment building in Greenwich Village. BILL gets out and pays his fare.

BILL

Keep the change. Merry Christmas.

BILL is carrying a small cake-box. The cab drives off as BILL walks up the stoop to the front door. He stands aside to let a parcel-laden lady go by, then goes in through the front door.

115. INT. LOBBY – DOMINO APARTMENT BUILDING – NIGHT

A shabby lobby. BILL walks up to the apartment door. He rings the bell. A woman's voice is heard from the other side of the door. This is SALLY.

> SALLY *(o/s)*
>
> Who is it?

> BILL
>
> Domino?

> SALLY *(o/s)*
>
> No, she's not in.

> BILL
>
> Er . . . are you expecting her back soon?

> SALLY *(o/s)*
>
> No, I'm not.

> BILL
>
> OK. I have something for her. Can I leave this with you?

                    SALLY *(o/s)*
Just a minute. . . .

The door is unlocked and SALLY's face appears. BILL
gives her the cake box.

                    SALLY
                (taking box)
Can I say who it's from?

                    BILL
Well, just tell her it's from Bill.

                    SALLY
You're Bill . . . *the* Bill? You're the doctor who
was here last night?

                    BILL
Well, I suppose I am.

                    SALLY
Domino said how nice you were to her.

                    BILL
Did she?

                    SALLY
Uh-huh. Why don't you come in for a second?

BILL

Sure.

BILL enters the apartment.

116. INT. DOMINO APARTMENT – NIGHT

SALLY closes and locks the door. She is very attractive, about DOMINO's age, and she signals to BILL to go into the kitchen. As he enters he stops and turns.

SALLY, who likes the look of him, puts the cake on the table and blatantly pushes herself up against him.

SALLY

I'm Sally.

BILL

Hello, Sally.

BILL, taking off his overcoat, is not reticent in returning the advance.

SALLY

Hi.

BILL

So, do you have any idea when you expect
Domino back?

SALLY

No, I have no idea.

BILL

You have no idea?

They are flirting heavily now.

SALLY

No. Well, to be perfectly honest, she . . . she may
not even be coming back.

BILL
(laughs)

She may not even be coming back?

*Excited by their closeness, BILL starts to fondle SALLY's
breast.*

SALLY

Well, umm . . . I, erh. . . .

BILL

You, erh. . . .

SALLY
(awkwardly)

I think some . . . something that I should tell
you.

BILL

Really?

SALLY

Yeah . . . but I don't know.

BILL

You don't know? What is it?

SALLY is very taken by the advance from BILL, but forces herself to talk.

SALLY

I don't know whether to tell you this. Oh, well
. . . why don't you . . . why don't you have a
seat?

(pause)

OK, let's sit down.

They separate and sit at each end of the kitchen table. BILL laughs at SALLY's difficulty in saying what is on her mind.

SALLY

Oh . . . I don't quite know how to say this.

BILL

You don't quite know how?

SALLY

Well, considering that you were with Domino
last night . . .

BILL

Hmm. . . .

SALLY

(very awkwardly)

I think it would be only fair to you, to let you
know that, umm . . . she got the results of a
blood test this morning and, erh . . . it was HIV
positive.

BILL is taken aback. He was not expecting news like
this.

BILL

HIV positive?

SALLY

Yeah.

BILL doesn't know what to say.

BILL

Well, I am very . . . very sorry to hear that.

SALLY

Yeah, I mean, it's absolutely devastating.

Both of them sit there, lost for something to say. SALLY
tries to snap out of it.

SALLY
(breezily)
Listen, can I offer you anything? Cup of coffee
maybe?

BILL
No thank you. I think erh . . . maybe I had better
be going.

117. EXT. STREET – SOHO – NIGHT

It is deserted, but for a passing car, as we see BILL
slowly walking down the street.

118. EXT. ANOTHER STREET – SOHO – NIGHT

BILL, hands thrust deep in his pockets, becomes aware
of somebody else walking behind him. He looks back and
sees a figure keeping a distance on the opposite side of
the street. BILL realizes he is being followed. This is the
STALKER.

119. EXT. ANOTHER STREET – GREENWICH
VILLAGE – NIGHT

BILL turns a corner and checks behind him. He contin-
ues down the street and looks back.

The STALKER, though keeping his distance, has now crossed to BILL's side of the street. He's a heavy set guy with a shaved head.

BILL, now worried, tries to hail a cab, but none stop. Then he sees a taxi pull up and someone gets out. BILL runs across to grab the cab and starts to open the door.

BILL

Taxi.

DRIVER

Off duty.

The cab pulls away, leaving BILL at the curbside.

BILL tries to see if the STALKER is still following him and then decides to continue walking. As he reaches a newspaper kiosk he sees the STALKER come round the corner and stop. BILL stops too and looks at him for some time while wondering what will happen next.

BILL then picks up a copy of the New York Post *and throws some change down. The STALKER crosses the street, all the time keeping a steady watch on BILL. Then he stops and BILL waits. Finally, after a stand-off, the STALKER walks away leaving BILL feeling very anxious.*

BILL turns and walks down the street. He sees Sharkey's Café and welcomes the security the company of other people will afford him.

120. INT. PASSAGEWAY – SHARKEY'S CAFÉ – NIGHT

BILL walks up the stairs and into the café.

121. INT. SHARKEY'S CAFÉ – NIGHT

BILL enters. Mozart's Requiem *is playing and the place is full of people. He goes to the counter and a friendly waitress looks up.*

BILL

I'll just have a cappuccino, please.

WAITRESS

I'll bring it over to you.

BILL sees a table at the other end of the room and goes across to it. He sits down and opens the New York Post *and glances agitatedly out of the café windows.*

Suddenly, something in the paper catches his eye: a headline which reads, EX-BEAUTY QUEEN IN HOTEL DRUGS OVERDOSE. He reads the article in dread of what it seems to be revealing.

122. EXT. HOSPITAL – NEW YORK – NIGHT

A busy Manhattan general hospital: ambulances, cars, staff and public.

123. INT. MAIN ENTRANCE – HOSPITAL – NIGHT

Through the revolving glass doors, we see a cab pull up outside. BILL gets out and walks through the revolving door and up to the reception desk.

                    BILL
Good evening.

                 RECEPTIONIST
Good evening.

                    BILL
I'm Dr Harford. One of my patients was
admitted earlier this morning, a Miss Amanda
Curran. Could you please give me her room
number?

                 RECEPTIONIST
        (keyboarding a computer terminal)
Certainly. Her name again?

                    BILL
Curran. Amanda Curran.

*The RECEPTIONIST checks the spelling as she enters the
name on the computer.*

                 RECEPTIONIST
    C . . . U . . . R . . . R . . . A . . . N?

                    BILL
Yes.

RECEPTIONIST

Miss Amanda Curran?

BILL

That's right.

RECEPTIONIST

I'm sorry, doctor, Miss Curran died this afternoon.

BILL

She died this afternoon?

RECEPTIONIST

Yes, at three-forty-five p.m. I'm sorry.

124. INT. CORRIDOR – HOSPITAL – NIGHT

BILL follows an ORDERLY down the corridor.

125. INT. MORGUE – HOSPITAL – NIGHT

The ORDERLY leads BILL into the morgue and then walks over to a bank of refrigerated body drawers and pulls out a body on a tray. He steps back.

BILL stands looking at the corpse – we recognize her as the woman we saw at ZIEGLER's party, the one who had over-dosed in the bathroom, MANDY.

BILL leans closer to study her face. He moves around

*to her head. He leans forward, bringing his face close to
hers, and closes his eyes. It's as if he were going to kiss
her. He stops short and slowly pulls back until he is looking down at her face.*

126. INT. ANOTHER CORRIDOR – HOSPITAL –
NIGHT

*Despondently, BILL walks down the corridor. His mo-
bile phone rings. He takes it out of his pocket.*

> BILL
> Hello? Yes, it's Dr Harford . . . Tonight? . . . No,
> no, no. That's OK. Just, please, tell him that I'll
> be there in about twenty minutes . . . OK?

127. EXT. ZIEGLER MANSION – NIGHT

Lights burning in most rooms. Night traffic.

128. INT. CORRIDOR/ HALL – ZIEGLER MANSION –
NIGHT

*HARRIS, ZIEGLER's personal assistant, leads BILL
down the corridor and across the hall. Not a word is
spoken. They come to a door and HARRIS knocks on it.*

129. INT. BILLIARD ROOM – ZIEGLER MANSION –
NIGHT

*A big, pine paneled room, lined with books and antique
artifacts. In the middle of the room ZIEGLER is alone,
playing shots on the billiard table. ZIEGLER hears the
knock, puts the cue down and walks across the room to
the door.*

ZIEGLER
(calling out)

Come in.

*HARRIS opens the door, lets BILL in and closes the door
immediately after.*

ZIEGLER
Bill, I appreciate you coming.

BILL

Sure.

ZIEGLER
Sorry to drag you over tonight. Let me have
your coat.

BILL
(removing over-coat)
No, no. I . . . I was out anyway, thank you.

                    ZIEGLER
How about a drink?

ZIEGLER gives BILL a friendly slap on the shoulder as he takes his coat.

                    BILL
Are you having one?

                    ZIEGLER
Sure.

They walk over to the drinks table. ZIEGLER laying BILL's coat over an armchair.

                    BILL
OK.

                    ZIEGLER
What would you like?

                    BILL
Just a little scotch.

                    ZIEGLER
Good. How do you take it? Neat?

ZIEGLER pours the drinks.

BILL

Please. That was a terrific party the other night.
Alice and I had a wonderful time.

ZIEGLER

Well, good, good. It was great seeing you both.
Cheers.

*They "clink" glasses and ZIEGLER leads BILL over to
the billiard table.*

BILL

Cheers. Were you playing?

ZIEGLER

No. Just knocking a few balls around.

*They face each other across the table as BILL takes a
drink.*

BILL

Beautiful scotch.

ZIEGLER

That's a twenty-five-year-old. I'll send you over
a case.

BILL

No, please.

ZIEGLER

Sure, why not?

BILL

No . . . no!

ZIEGLER

You, erh . . . do you feel like playing?

ZIEGLER starts playing with a billiard ball. He looks particularly ill at ease.

BILL

No thanks . . . you go ahead. I'll watch.

ZIEGLER

No, no, no, no, no, no. I . . . I was just, erh. . . .
Listen, Bill, the reason I asked you to come
over, I, I . . . I need to talk to you about
something.

BILL

Sure.

ZIEGLER

It's a little bit awkward. And I have to be
completely frank.

                    BILL

What kind of problem are you having?

                  ZIEGLER

It isn't a medical problem.

ZIEGLER slowly walks around the table towards BILL.

                  ZIEGLER

Actually, it concerns you, Bill . . . I . . . I know
what happened last night. And I know what's
been going on since then. And I think you just
might . . . have the wrong idea about one or two
things.

                    BILL

I'm sorry, Victor, I . . . what in the hell are you
talking about?

                  ZIEGLER

Please, Bill, no games. I was there, at the house.
I saw everything that went on. Bill, what the
hell did you think you were doing?

ZIEGLER picks up his glass and starts to pace the floor.

                  ZIEGLER

I couldn't, I couldn't even begin to, to imagine
how, how you had even heard about it, let alone

got yourself through the door. And then I
remembered seeing you with that . . . that . . .
that prick piano player . . . Nick whatever-the-
fuck his name was at my party. It didn't take
much to figure out the rest.

BILL stares at the table in embarrassment.

                    BILL
It wasn't Nick's fault. It was mine.

                    ZIEGLER
                (still pacing)
Of course it was Nick's fault. If he hadn't
mentioned it to you in the first place, none of
this would have happened. I recommended that
little cocksucker to those people and he's made
me look like a complete asshole.

                    BILL
Victor, what can I say? I had . . . absolutely no
idea you were involved in any way.

ZIEGLER leans on the table trying to gain composure.

                    ZIEGLER
I know you didn't, Bill. But I also know that you
. . . you went to Nick's hotel this morning and
talked to the desk clerk.

BILL

How do you know that?

ZIEGLER

Because I had you followed.

BILL "snorts" a short laugh in response.

BILL

You had me *followed*?

Now it is ZIEGLER's turn to be embarrassed.

ZIEGLER

I . . . OK, OK! I'm sorry all right. I owe you an
apology, I . . . this was for your own good,
believe me. Now look, I know what the desk
clerk told you but what he didn't tell you is that
all they did was put Nick on a plane to Seattle.
By now he's probably back with his family . . .
probably banging Mrs Nick.

*ZIEGLER's attempt to lighten the conversation falls flat
with BILL.*

BILL

The clerk said he had a bruise on his face.

ZIEGLER moves closer to BILL and sits on the table.

ZIEGLER

OK, he had a bruise on his face. That's a hell of
a lot less than he deserves. Listen, Bill. I don't
think you realize what sort of trouble you were
in last night.

*ZIEGLER gets off the table, picks up BILL's glass and
walks to the drinks table.*

ZIEGLER

What do you think those people were? They
weren't just ordinary people there. If I told you
their names . . . I'm not gonna tell you their
names, but if I did, I don't think you'd sleep so
well.

BILL

Was it the second password? Is that what gave
me away?

*ZIEGLER pours more scotch for BILL and himself and
puts BILL's glass on the billiard table. ZIEGLER then
walks over to an armchair on the other side of the room.*

ZIEGLER

Yes, finally. But not because you didn't know it
. . . it's because there was no second password.

ZIEGLER sits down in the armchair.

ZIEGLER

Of course, it didn't help a whole lot . . . those
people arrive in limos and you showed up in a
taxi. Or, that when they took your coat, they
found the receipt from the rental house in your
pocket, made out to you-know-who. . . .

*BILL moves away and turns his back on ZIEGLER. He
feels very awkward.*

BILL

There was a . . . there was a . . . there was a
woman there, who, erh . . . tried to warn me.

ZIEGLER

I know. . . .

BILL

Do you know who she was?

*ZIEGLER gets up and goes near to where BILL stands
with his back still turned. He puts his glass on the edge
of the table.*

ZIEGLER

Yes . . . she was . . . she was a hooker. Sorry, but
that's what she was.

BILL moves away, still with his back to ZIEGLER and sits in an armchair. He runs his hand through his hair, trying to figure everything out.

BILL

A hooker?

ZIEGLER

Bill, suppose I told you that . . . that everything that happened to you there, the threats, the girls . . . warnings, the last minute interventions . . . suppose I said all of that was staged, that it was a kind of charade? That it was fake?

BILL

Fake?

ZIEGLER

Yes, fake.

BILL
(not understanding)
Why would they do that?

ZIEGLER

Why? In plain words, to scare the living shit out of you. To keep you quiet about where you'd been and what you'd seen.

BILL takes the article he tore out of the New York Post *in Sharkey's Café and hands it to ZIEGLER who looks at it.*

BILL

Have you seen this?

ZIEGLER

Yes, I have.

He folds it and gives it back to BILL.

BILL

I saw her body, in the morgue. Was she . . . was she the woman at the party?

ZIEGLER, hands in pockets, moves away to the billiard table.

ZIEGLER

Yes, she was.

BILL, in an attempt to put everything together, gets up and walks away from ZIEGLER as if to put some distance between them.

BILL

Victor, the woman lying dead in the morgue was the woman at the party?

ZIEGLER

Yes.

BILL, getting very upset, turns round on ZIEGLER.

BILL

Well, Victor, maybe I'm . . . missing something
here. You called it a fake, charade. Do you mind
telling me what kind of fucking charade ends
with somebody turning up dead?

ZIEGLER
(rising anger)

OK, Bill. Let's . . . let's . . . let's . . . let's cut the
bullshit, all right? You've been way out of your
depth for the last twenty-four hours. You
wanna know what kinda charade? I'll tell you
exactly what kind. That whole play-acted "take
me" phony sacrifice that you've been jerking
yourself off with had absolutely nothing to do
with her real death. Nothing happened to her
after you left that party that hadn't happened
to her before. She got her brains fucked out.
Period.
(pause)

When they took her home she was just fine and
the rest of it's right there in the paper. She was
a junky. She OD'd. There was nothing
suspicious. Her door was locked from the
inside. The police are happy. End of story.
(pause)

Come on . . . it was always just gonna be a
matter of time with her. Remember, you told
her so yourself? Remember the one with the
great tits who OD'd in my bathroom?

*BILL hangs his head as he recollects that it was indeed
what he'd told ZIEGLER and MANDY at the party after
the "bathroom incident."*

*BILL slowly moves away as ZIEGLER, trying to mol-
lify him, walks up behind him.*

ZIEGLER
Listen, Bill. Nobody killed anybody. Someone
died. It happens all the time. Life goes on. It
always does until it doesn't.

*ZIEGLER lays his hands on BILL's shoulders in a
friendly reassuring way.*

ZIEGLER
But you know that, don't you?

130. INT. BEDROOM – BILL & ALICE'S
APARTMENT – NIGHT

*The mask that BILL wore at the ball rests on a pillow
bathed in moonlight. Next to it lies ALICE asleep.*

131. INT. HALLWAY – BILL & ALICE'S
APARTMENT – NIGHT

*The front door opens and a totally dejected BILL enters.
He slowly walks down the hallway, takes off his over-*

coat and just dumps it on a chair. He walks across the living room towards the illuminated Christmas tree. He pauses to look at the tree then switches its lights off.

BILL takes off his jacket and hangs it over the back of a chair. Tired and exhausted he walks, dejectedly, into the kitchen, loosening his tie. He goes to the fridge and takes out a can of beer. Then he goes to the table, slumps down into a chair and starts to drink.

132. INT. BEDROOM – BILL & ALICE'S APARTMENT – NIGHT

BILL quietly opens the bedroom door. To his dismay, he sees the mask on the pillow next to ALICE. BILL, emotionally wrecked, walks slowly towards the bed and sits down with tears in his eyes. Finally, he can restrain himself no longer, and breaks down into uncontrollable sobbing.

ALICE wakes to see BILL's complete helplessness as he collapses and lays his head on her breast. She puts an arm around him as he sobs.

BILL
I'll tell you everything. I'll tell you everything.

133. INT. LIVING ROOM – BILL & ALICE'S APARTMENT – DAY

Dawn has given way to early morning. ALICE, cigarette in hand, sits in tearful silence as she contemplates what

BILL has told her. She looks at BILL who sits on the sofa opposite looking ashamed, humiliated, remorseful. ALICE, trying to constrain her disappointment, remembers what they have to do this day.

ALICE

Helena's gonna be up soon. She's uh . . . she's expecting us to take her Christmas shopping today.

134. INT. TOY STORE – DAY

BILL and ALICE walk together with HELENA who is trying to catch the soap bubbles floating in the air above her. Then HELENA runs off as BILL and ALICE follow, BILL glancing anxiously at ALICE as they go. They catch up with HELENA as she looks at a toy pram.

ALICE

That's nice.

HELENA

I could put Sabrina in here.

ALICE

Yeah.

HELENA

It's really . . . pretty.

> ALICE

It's old fashioned.

HELENA runs off again and when BILL and ALICE catch up with her, they see she has discovered a huge teddy bear.

> ALICE

He's big.

> HELENA

I hope Santa Claus gets me one of these for Christmas!

> ALICE

You do?

> HELENA

Yes.

> ALICE

Well, you're gonna have to wait and see.

HELENA runs off again, and BILL and ALICE follow, each with everything to say but no way of saying it until BILL plucks up the courage to speak.

BILL

Alice . . . what do you think we should do?

They stop and ALICE tries to gather her thoughts.

ALICE

What do I think we should do?

HELENA

Look, Mommy.

BILL and ALICE look at HELENA who holds up a fairy doll. They smile at her.

ALICE

Oh . . . what do I think? I dunno. I mean,
maybe . . .

They move away into an aisle where ALICE stops and begins to explain her feelings. HELENA walks between them which brings ALICE to a halt.

ALICE
(to Helena)

Hey!

When she thinks HELENA is out of earshot, ALICE continues, searching for words.

ALICE

Maybe, I think, we should be grateful . . .
grateful that we've managed to survive through
all of our adventures, whether they were real
or only a dream.

BILL
(moving closer)
Are you . . . are you sure of that?

ALICE

Am . . . am I sure? Umm . . . only . . . only as
sure as I am that the reality of one night, let
alone that of a whole life time, can ever be the
whole truth.

BILL

And no dream is ever just a dream.

ALICE

Hmm . . . The important thing is we're awake
now and hopefully for a long time to come.

BILL

Forever.

ALICE

Forever?

BILL

Forever.

ALICE

Let's . . . let's not use that word, it frightens me.
But I do love you and you know there is
something very important we need to do as
soon as possible?

BILL

What's that?

ALICE

Fuck.

[FINIS]

CREDITS AND CAST

Produced and Directed by   STANLEY KUBRICK

Screenplay by   STANLEY KUBRICK and
FREDERIC RAPHAEL

Inspired by "Traumnovelle" by   ARTHUR SCHNITZLER

Executive Producer   JAN HARLAN

Co-Producer   BRIAN W. COOK

Assistant to the Director   LEON VITALI

Lighting Cameraman   LARRY SMITH

Production Designers   LES TOMKINS
ROY WALKER

Editor   NIGEL GALT

Original Music by   JOCELYN POOK

GYÖRGY LIGETI
Musica Ricercata II
DOMINIC HARLAN, piano

DMITRI SHOSTAKOVICH
from Jazz Suite, Waltz 2
Royal Concertgebouw Orchestra
conducted by Riccardo Chailly

CHRIS ISAAK
"Baby Did A Bad Bad Thing"

Costume Designer   MARIT ALLEN

Costume Supervisor   NANCY THOMPSON

Wardrobe Mistress   JACQUELINE DURRAN

Hair by   KERRY WARN

Make-Up   ROBERT McCANN

Sound Recordist   EDWARD TISE

Supervising Sound Editor   PAUL CONWAY

Sound Maintenance   TONY BELL

Re-Recording Mixers   GRAHAM V.
HARTSTONE, A.M.P.S.
MICHAEL A. CARTER
NIGEL GALT
ANTHONY CLEAL

Production Manager	MARGARET ADAMS
Script Supervisor	ANN SIMPSON
Assistant to Stanley Kubrick	ANTHONY FREWIN
Casting	DENISE CHAMIAN
	LEON VITALI
First Assistant Director	BRIAN W. COOK
Second Assistant Director	ADRIAN TOYNTON
Third Assistant Directors	BECKY HUNT
	RHUN FRANCIS
Location Managers	SIMON McNAIR SCOTT
	ANGUS MORE GORDON
Location Research	MANUEL HARLAN
Location Assistant	TOBIN HUGHES
Supervising Art Director	KEVIN PHIPPS
Art Director	JOHN FENNER
Draughtsperson	STEPHEN DOBRIC
Draughtsperson	JON BILLINGTON
Assistant Draughtsperson	PIPPA RAWLINSON
Art Department Assistants	SAMANTHA JONES
	KIRA-ANNE PELICAN
Original Paintings	CHRISTIANE KUBRICK
	KATHARINA HOBBS
Venetian Masks Research	BARBARA DEL GRECO
Production Accountant	JOHN TREHY
Assistant Accountant	LARA SARGENT
Accounts Assistants	MATTHEW DALTON
	STELLA WYCHERLEY
Set Decorators	TERRY WELLS Snr
	LISA LEONE
Production Buyers	MICHAEL KING
	JEANNE VERTIGAN
	SOPHIE BATSFORD
First Assistant Editor	MELANIE VINER
	CUNEO
Avid Assistant Editor	CLAUS WEHLISCH
Assistant Editor	CLAIRE FERGUSON
Foley Editor	BECKI PONTING
Assistant Sound Editor	IAIN EYRE

Steadicam Operators	ELIZABETH ZIEGLER
	PETER CAVACIUTI
Camera Operator	MARTIN HUME
Focus Pullers	RAWDON HAYNE
	NICK PENN
	JASON WRENN
Clapper Loaders	CRAIG BLOOR
	KEITH ROBERTS
Camera Grips	WILLIAM GEDDES
	ANDY HOPKINS
Back Projection Supervisor	CHARLES STAFFELL
Camera Technical Advisor	JOE DUNTON
Translights	STILLED MOVIE LTD
Translight Photography	GERARD MAGUIRE
Stills Photography	MANUEL HARLAN
Video Co-Ordinator	ANDREW HADDOCK
Video Assistant	MARTIN WARD
Gaffers	RONNIE PHILLIPS
	PAUL TOOMEY
Best Boy	MICHAEL WHITE
Electricians	RON EMERY
	JOE ALLEN
	SHAWN WHITE
	DEAN WILKINSON
Production Associate	MICHAEL DOVEN
Choreographer	YOLANDE SNAITH
Dialect Coach to Ms. Kidman	ELIZABETH
	HIMELSTEIN
Assistants to Ms. Kidman	ANDREA DOVEN
	KERRY DAVID
Assistant to Mr. Kubrick	EMILIO D'ALESSANDRO
Chargehand Standby Propman	JAKE WELLS
Standby Propman	JOHN O'CONNELL
Property Master	TERRY WELLS Jnr
Property Storeman	KEN BACON
Dressing Propmen	TODD QUATTROMINI
	GERALD O'CONNOR
Production Co-Ordinator	KATE GARBETT
Unit Nurse	CLAIRE LITCHFIELD

Catering	LOCATION CATERERS LTD
Security	ALAN REID
Extras Casting	20-20 PRODUCTIONS LTD
Medical Advisor	DR. C.J. SCHEINER MD PhD
Journalistic Advisor	LARRY CELONA
Secretary	RACHEL HUNT
Computer Assistant	NICK FREWIN
Production Assistant	TRACEY CRAWLEY
Construction Manager	JOHN MAHER
Standby Carpenter	ROY HANSFORD
Standby Stagehand	DESMOND O'BOY
Standby Painter	STEVE CLARK
Standby Rigger	ANTHONY RICHARDS
Action Vehicle Mechanic	TOM WATSON
Action Vehicle Co-Ordinator	MARTIN WARD
Equipment Vehicles	LAYS INTERNATIONAL LTD
Facility Vehicles	LOCATION FACILITIES LTD
Action Vehicles	DREAM CARS
Facilities Supervisor	DAVID JONES
Fire Cover	FIRST UNIT FIRE & SAFETY LTD

SECOND UNIT

Production Manager	LISA LEONE
Cinematography	PATRICK TURLEY MALIK SAYEED ARTHUR JAFFA
Steadicam Operator	JIM C. McCONKEY
Grip	DONAVAN C. LAMBERT
Camera Assistants	CARLOS OMAR GUERRA JONAS STEADMAN
Production Assistant	NELSON PEÑA

CAST IN ORDER OF APPEARANCE

Dr William Harford	TOM CRUISE
Alice Harford	NICOLE KIDMAN
Helena Harford	MADISON EGINTON
Roz	JACKIE SAWIRIS
Victor Ziegler	SYDNEY POLLACK
Ilona	LESLIE LOWE
Bandleader	PETER BENSON
Nick Nightingale	TODD FIELD
Ziegler's Secretary	MICHAEL DOVEN
Sandor Szavost	SKY DUMONT
Gayle	LOUISE TAYLOR
Nuala	STEWART THORNDIKE
Harris	RANDALL PAUL
Mandy	JULIENNE DAVIS
Lisa	LISA LEONE
Lou Nathanson	KEVIN CONNEALY
Marion	MARIE RICHARDSON
Carl	THOMAS GIBSON
Rosa	MARIANA HEWETT
Rowdy College Kids	DAN ROLLMAN
	GAVIN PERRY
	CHRIS PARE
	ADAM LIAS
	CHRISTIAN CLARKE
	KYLE WHITCOMBE
Naval Officer	GARY GOBA
Domino	VINESSA SHAW
Maître D'—Café Sonata	FLORIAN WINDORFER
Milich	RADE SHERBEDGIA
Japanese Man #1	TOGO IGAWA
Japanese Man #2	EIJI KUSUHARA
Milich's Daughter	LEELEE SOBIESKI
Cab Driver	SAM DOUGLAS
Gateman #1	ANGUS MacINNES
Mysterious Woman	ABIGAIL GOOD

Tall Butler	BRIAN W. COOK
Red Cloak	LEON VITALI
Waitress at Gillespie's	CARMELA MARNER
Desk Clerk	ALAN CUMMING
Sally	FAY MASTERSON
Stalker	PHIL DAVIES
Girl at Sharkey's	CINDY DOLENC
Hospital Receptionist	CLARKE HAYES
Morgue Orderly	TREVA ETIENNE

MASKED PARTY PRINCIPALS
(IN ALPHABETICAL ORDER)

COLIN ANGUS	LEE HENSHAW
KARLA ASHLEY	ATEEKA POOLE
KATHRYN CHARMAN	ADAM PUDNEY
JAMES DEMARIA	SHARON QUINN
ANTHONY DESERGIO	BEN DE SAUSMARCZ
JANIE DICKENS	EMMA LOU SHARRATT
LAURA FALLACE	PAUL SPELLING
VANESSA FENTON	MATTHEW THOMPSON
GEORGINA FINCH	DAN TRAVERS
PETER GODWIN	RUSSELL TRIGG
ABIGAIL GOOD	KATE WHALIN
JOANNA HEATH	

DREAM STORY

Twenty-four brown slaves rowed the splendid galley that would bring Prince Amgiad to the Calif's palace. But the Prince, wrapped in his purple cloak, lay alone on the deck beneath the deep blue, star-spangled night sky, and his gaze—"

Up to this point the little girl had been reading aloud; now, quite suddenly, her eyes closed. Her parents looked at each other with a smile, and Fridolin bent over her, kissed her flaxen hair, and snapped shut the book that was resting on the table which had not as yet been cleared. The child looked up as if caught out.

"Nine o'clock," said her father, "time for bed." And as Albertine too had now bent over the child, the parents' hands touched as they fondly stroked her brow, and with a tender smile that was no longer intended solely for the child, their eyes met. The maid came in, and bade the little one say goodnight to her parents; obediently she got up, proffered her lips to her father and mother to be kissed, and let the maid escort her quietly from the room. Left alone under the reddish glow of the hanging lamp, Fridolin and Albertine suddenly felt impelled to resume the discussion of their experiences at yesterday's masked ball which they had begun before the evening meal.

It had been their first ball of the year, which they had decided to attend just before the close of the carnival season. Immediately upon entering the ball-room, Fridolin had been greeted like an impatiently awaited friend by two dominoes dressed in red, whom he had not managed to identify, even though they were remarkably well informed about various epi-sodes from his hospital and student days. They had left the box to which they had invited him with such auspicious friendliness, promising shortly to return unmasked, but then had stayed away so long that he became impatient and decided to return to the ground floor, hoping to meet the two enigmatic creatures there again. He looked around intently, without how-ever catching sight of them; instead, quite unexpect-edly, another female reveller took him by the arm: it was his wife who had just withdrawn rather abruptly from a stranger, whose blasé melancholy air and foreign-sounding—evidently Polish—accent had at first intrigued her, but who had then suddenly let slip a surprisingly crude and insolent remark that had hurt and even frightened her. And so man and wife, glad at heart to have escaped a disappointingly banal charade, were soon sitting at the bar, like two lovers among other amorous couples, and chatting amiably over oysters and champagne, as though they had just become acquainted in some gallant comedy of seduc-tion, resistance and fulfilment; and then, after a swift coach-ride through the white winter's night, they sank into one another's arms with an ardour they had not experienced for quite some time. A grey morning awoke them all too soon. The husband's profession summoned him to his patients' bedside at an early hour, and the duties of housekeeper and mother did not allow Albertine to rest much longer. And so the hours had passed predictably and soberly enough in work and routine chores, and the events of the previous night from first to last had faded; and only now that both their days' work was over, the child asleep, and no further disturbance anticipated, did the shadowy figures from the masked ball, the melancholy stranger and the dominoes in red revive; and those trivial encounters became magically and painfully interfused with the treacherous illusion of missed opportunities. Innocent yet ominous questions and vague ambiguous answers passed to and fro between them; and as neither of them doubted the other's absolute candour, both felt the need for mild revenge. They exaggerated the extent to which their masked partners had attracted them, made fun of the jealous stirrings the other revealed, and lied dismissively about their own. Yet this light banter about the trivial adventures of the previous night led to more serious discussion of those hidden, scarcely admitted desires which are apt to raise dark and perilous storms even in the purest, most transparent soul; and they talked about those secret regions for which they felt scarcely any longing, yet towards which the irrational winds of fate might one day drive them, if only in their dreams. For however much they might belong to one another heart and soul, they knew last night was not the first time they had been stirred by a whiff of freedom, danger and adventure; and with self-tormenting anxiety and sordid curiosity each sought to coax admissions from the other, and while drawing closer in their fear, each groped for any fact, however slight, any experience, however trivial, which might articulate the inexpressible, and frank confession of which might perhaps release them from a tension and mistrust that were slowly starting to become intolerable. Whether it was because she was the more impetuous, the more honest or the more warm-hearted, Albertine was the first to find the courage to make a frank confession; and with a trembling voice she asked Fridolin whether he remembered a young man the previous summer on the Danish coast, who had been sitting with two officers at the table next to them one evening, and on receiving a telegram during the meal had promptly taken a hasty leave of his two friends.

Fridolin nodded. "What about him?" he asked.

"That same morning I had seen him once before," replied Albertine, "as he was hurrying up the hotel stairs with his yellow suitcase. He had glanced at me as we passed, but a few steps further up he stopped, turned round towards me and our eyes could not help meeting. He did not smile, indeed his face seemed to cloud over, and I must have reacted likewise, because I felt moved as never before. The whole day I lay on the beach lost in dreams. Were he to summon me—or so I believed—I would not have been able to resist. I believed myself capable of doing anything; I felt I had as good as resolved to relinquish you, the child, my future, yet at the same time—will you believe this?— you were more dear to me than ever. It was that same afternoon, you remember, that we talked so confidingly about a thousand things, discussing our future together, discussing the child as we had not done for ages. Then at sunset when we were sitting on the balcony, he walked past us on the beach below without looking up, and I was overjoyed to see him. But it was you whose brow I stroked and hair I kissed, and in my love for you there was also a good deal of distressing pity. That evening I wore a white rose in my belt, and you yourself said that I looked very beautiful. Perhaps it was no coincidence that the stranger was sitting near us with his friends. He did not look across at me, but I toyed with the idea of stepping over to his table and saying to him: Here I am, my long awaited one, my beloved—take me away. At that moment they brought him the telegram; he read it, went pale, whispered a few words to the younger of the two officers, and with an enigmatic look in my direction left the room."

"And then?" asked Fridolin dryly as she fell silent.

"Nothing more. All I know is that next morning I awoke in some trepidation. What I was anxious about—whether it was that he had left, or that he might still be there—I do not know, and even then I did not know. Yet when at noon he still had not appeared, I heaved a sigh of relief. Don't question me further, Fridolin, I have told you the whole truth.— You too had some sort of experience on that beach—of that I'm certain."

Fridolin got up, paced up and down the room a few times, then said: "You're right." He stood at the window, his face in darkness. "In the morning," he began in a restrained, somewhat resentful tone, "often very early before you got up, I would wander along the shore out past the resort; yet early as it was, the sun would always be shining brightly over the sea. Out there along the shore, as you know, there were little houses, each a little world unto its own, some with fenced-off gardens, some just surrounded by woods, and the bathing-huts were separated from the houses by the road and by a stretch of sand. I seldom encountered anybody, and there were never any bathers at that hour. One morning, however, I suddenly became aware of a female figure, not visible before, who was gingerly advancing along the narrow side-walk of one of those bathing-huts on stilts, putting one foot in front of the other and stretching her arms behind her as she groped along the wooden wall. She was a young girl of no more than fifteen, her loose, flaxen hair falling over her shoulders and on one side across her tender breast. Gazing down into the water, she slowly inched her way with lowered eyes along the wall toward the near corner of the hut, and suddenly emerged directly opposite where I was standing: she reached behind her even further with her arms, as if to gain a firmer hold, looked up and suddenly caught sight of me. Her whole body began to tremble, as though she were about either to fall or to run away. But as she could only have proceeded very slowly along the narrow plank, she decided not to move,— and so she just stood there, looking at first frightened, then angry and finally embarrassed. But then all at once she smiled, a ravishing smile; indeed there was a welcoming twinkle in her eye,—and at the same time a gentle mockery about the way she lightly skimmed the water between us with her foot. Then she stretched her young, slender body, as though exulting in her beauty, and evidently proud and sweetly aroused at feeling my ardent gaze upon her. We stood opposite each other like this for perhaps ten seconds, with lips half open and eyes aflame. Involuntarily I stretched out my arms toward her; there was joy and abandon in her gaze. All at once, however, she shook her head vigorously, let go of the side of the hut with one hand, and peremptorily signalled that I should withdraw; and when I could not bring myself to obey at once, such a pleading, such a beseeching look came into her child's eyes that I had no alternative but to turn away. I hastily resumed my walk without once turning round—less out of consideration, obedience or chivalry, than because I had felt so profoundly moved by her parting look—far transcending anything I had experienced before—that I was on the point of swooning." And with that he ended.

"And how often," asked Albertine flatly, looking straight ahead, "did you later follow the same path?"

"All I have told you," replied Fridolin, "just happened to occur on the last day of our stay in Denmark. Even I don't know how things might have developed under other circumstances. And you too, Albertine, shouldn't inquire any further."

He was still standing at the window, motionless. Albertine got up and went over to him, her eyes dark and moist, her brow slightly creased. "In future we should always tell each other things like this at once," she said.

He nodded silently.

"Promise me."

He drew her to him. "Do you really doubt that?" he asked; but his voice still sounded harsh.

She took his hands, fondled them and looked up at him with tearful eyes, in the depths of which he tried to read her thoughts. She was now thinking about the other, more real, experiences of his youth, some of which she was privy to, since during the first years of their marriage he had given way to her jealous curiosity rather too eagerly, and revealed, or, as it often seemed to him, surrendered many things he should perhaps have kept to himself. He could tell that various memories were now resurfacing within her with some urgency, and so he was hardly surprised when, as if in a dream, she mentioned the half-forgotten name of one of his youthful loves. Yet to him it came across as a reproach, even as a quiet threat.

He drew her hands to his lips.

"In every woman—believe me, even though it may sound trite,—in every woman whom I thought I was in love with, it was always you that I was searching for. I feel this more deeply, Albertine, than you can ever understand."

She smiled sadly. "And what if I too had chosen to go exploring first?" she said. Her expression changed, becoming inscrutable and cold. He let go her hands, as if he had caught her out in a lie or infidelity; but she continued, "Ah, if only you all knew," and again fell silent.

"If we only knew—? What do you mean by that?"

Rather harshly she replied: "More or less, my dear, what you imagine."

"Albertine—is there something you have never told me?"

She nodded with a strange smile and looked straight ahead. Vague irrational doubts began to stir within him.

"I don't quite understand," he said. "You were scarcely seventeen when we became engaged."

"Yes, Fridolin, a little over sixteen. And yet"—she looked him straight in the eye—"it was not my fault if I was still a virgin when I became your wife."

"Albertine—!" And she continued:

"It was on the Wörthersee, shortly before our engagement, Fridolin, when one beautiful summer evening an extremely handsome youth appeared outside my window which looked out over broad extensive meadows, we chatted away together and in the course of our conversation I thought to myself, just listen to what I thought: What a sweet, delightful, young person he is,—he would only have to say the word this minute, though of course it would have to be the right one, and I would go out and join him in the meadows and follow him wherever he desired,—into the wood perhaps;—or it would be lovelier still if we were to go out on to the lake together in a boat—and that night he could have everything he desired of me. Yes, that is what I thought to myself.—But he did not say the word, this charming youth; he just fondly kissed my hand,—and the next morning asked me whether I would be his wife. And I said yes."

Fridolin let her hand go, displeased. "And what if that evening," he remarked, "someone else had happened to stand outside your window, and had said the right word: for example—" he wondered whose name he should mention, but she stretched out her arm in a gesture of demurral.

"Anyone else, whoever it might have been, could have said what he liked, it would have been to little avail. And if you hadn't been the one to stand before my window"—she smiled up at him—"then the summer evening would not have been so lovely either."

His mouth twisted in a sneer. "That's what you say now, so at this moment you may even believe. But—"

There was a knock at the door. The chambermaid entered and announced that the porter's wife from the Schreivogelgasse had come to fetch the doctor on behalf of the Count Counsellor, who was again feeling very ill. Fridolin went out into the hall, learned from the messenger that the Count Counsellor had had another heart-attack and was in a bad way, and promised to come over at once.

"Are you going out?" Albertine asked him as he was hastily preparing to leave, and from her irritable tone it seemed as though he were deliberately treating her unjustly.

A little incredulously Fridolin answered, "But I have to."

She sighed lightly.

"It shouldn't be too bad, I hope," said Fridolin, "in the past, three grams of morphine have usually helped him over the attack."

The chambermaid had brought his fur coat, Fridolin kissed Albertine on the mouth and forehead a little absent-mindedly, as if the last hour's conversation had already been erased from his memory, and hurried off.

II

Out on the street he had to unbutton his fur coat. There had been a sudden thaw, the snow on the pavements had almost completely melted, and there was a breath of the coming spring in the air. From the Fridolins' apartment near the General Hospital in the Josefstadt it was barely a quarter of an hour's walk to the Schreivogelgasse; and so Fridolin soon found himself climbing the ill-lit, winding stairs of the old house to the second floor and tugging at the bell; but even before the old-fashioned tinkling resounded, he noticed that the door was ajar; he stepped through the unlit hall into the living-room and realized immediately that he had arrived too late. The green-shaded kerosene lamp hanging from the ceiling cast a dim light over the bed-cover, under which an emaciated body was stretched out motionless. The dead man's face was in shadow, but Fridolin knew it so well that he imagined he could see it quite distinctly—gaunt, wrinkled, the high forehead, the full short white beard, the strikingly ugly ears with their white hairs. The Court Counsellor's daughter, Marianne, sat at the foot of the bed, her arms hanging limply by her side as if in utter exhaustion. There was a smell of old furniture, medicaments, kerosene, the kitchen; also a whiff of eau de cologne and rose-water, and somehow Fridolin could even sense the stale sweetish smell of this pale girl, who though still young had for months, for years, been losing her bloom in the course of heavy household chores, tiring care and nocturnal vigils.

When the doctor entered, she had turned to look at him, but in the meagre light he could scarcely make out whether her cheeks turned red as they usually did when he appeared. She was on the point of getting up, but a gesture from Fridolin prevented her, and nodding, she greeted him with her large but sorrowful eyes. He approached the head of the bed, mechanically felt the dead man's temples, then his wrists which protruded from the wide, open sleeves resting on the bed-cover, then shrugged his shoulders in a mild gesture of regret, and put his hands in the pockets of his fur coat, his gaze wandering round the room and eventually coming to rest on Marianne. Her hair was thick and fair, but dry, her neck well-formed and slender, but of a yellowish complexion and no longer completely free of wrinkles, and her lips pinched as if from many unspoken words.

"Well now, my dear young lady," he said softly and almost in embarrassment, "you were scarcely unprepared for it."

She stretched out her hand toward him. He took it sympathically, asking dutifully about the last fatal attack, whereupon she related everything factually and briefly and then described the last relatively tranquil days during which Fridolin had not seen the sick man. Fridolin had drawn up a chair, seated himself opposite Marianne, and to console her intimated that in his last hour her father would hardly have suffered at all; then he enquired whether the relatives had been informed. Yes, the porter's wife was already on the way to her uncle, and in any case Dr Roediger would soon be there, "my fiancé," she added, and glanced at Fridolin's forehead rather than looking him in the eye.

Fridolin merely nodded. In the course of a year he had met Dr Roediger two or three times here in the house. This pale, excessively slim young man with glasses and a short blond beard, a lecturer in history at Vienna University, had made a favourable impression on him, without however rousing any further curiosity about him. Marianne would certainly look better, he thought, if she were his mistress. Her hair would be less dry, her lips redder and fuller. How old would she be? he then wondered. When I was first called out to the Court Counsellor's three or four years ago, she was twenty-three. Her mother was still alive then. She was more cheerful when her mother was alive. Didn't she take singing lessons for a while? So she is going to marry this lecturer. Why is she doing it? Certainly she is not in love with him and he can't have much money either. What sort of marriage will it turn out to be? Well, a marriage like a thousand others. What concern is it of mine? It is quite possible that I shall never see her again, since I will no longer have any function in this house. Ah, how many people I have never seen again, who were closer to me than she is.

While these thoughts were running through his head, Marianne had begun to talk about the dead man,—moreover with a certain urgency, as though by virtue of the mere fact of his death he had suddenly become a person of distinction. Was he really only fifty-four years old? Of course, the many worries and disappointments, his wife forever ailing,—and his son too had given him a great deal of trouble! What, she had a brother? Yes, of course! Surely she had told the doctor about him once before. The brother was now living abroad somewhere, and hanging up in Marianne's bedroom was a picture he had painted at fifteen. It showed an officer galloping down a hill. Her father had always pretended not to notice this painting. But it was a good painting. Her brother might have gone a long way under more favourable circumstances.

How excitedly she talks, thought Fridolin, and how her eyes are sparkling. Fever perhaps? Quite possibly. She has grown thinner recently. Probably acute bronchitis.

She talked on and on, but to him it seemed as if she did not really know whom she was talking to, or as if she were talking to herself. For twelve years now her brother had been away from home, indeed she had still been a child when he had suddenly disappeared. It would be four years ago at Christmas since they had last received news of him from some small Italian town. Strange, she had forgotten its name.

She continued talking thus a while aimlessly and almost without logical connection about indifferent matters, then suddenly she stopped and sat there silently, her head in her hands. Fridolin was tired and even more bored, and waited anxiously for the relatives or the fiancé to come. The silence in the room became oppressive. He felt as though the dead man were joining in their silence, not because he could no longer talk, but deliberately and out of sheer malice.

And with a sidelong glance at him Fridolin said: "At least as things stand, Marianne, you won't have to remain in this apartment much longer,"—and as she raised her head a little, without however looking up at Fridolin, he continued, "No doubt your fiancé will soon be offered a professorship; the situation in the Humanities is in that respect much more propitious than with us."—He reflected that years ago he too had aspired to an academic career, but that with his preference for a comfortable existence he had in the end decided to pursue the more practical side of his profession;—and suddenly he saw himself in relation to the excellent Dr Roediger as the lesser man.

"We will be moving in the autumn," said Marianne without stirring, "he has received an offer from Göttingen." "Ah," said Fridolin and wanted to congratulate her in some way, but this seemed hardly the appropriate moment under the circumstances. He glanced at the closed window and, as if exercising his prerogative as a physician, opened both wings without asking her permission and let in the breeze, which having by now become even warmer and more spring-like, seemed to bring with it a mild fragrance from the distant wakening woods. When he turned back toward the room, he saw Marianne's eyes turned toward him questioningly. He moved closer to her and remarked: "The fresh air will do you good, I hope. It has become quite warm, and last night"—he was going to say: we drove home from the masked ball in a flurry of snow, but he hastily reformulated his sentence and concluded: "Last night the snow in the streets was still half a meter deep."

She scarcely heard what he was saying. Her eyes grew moist, large tears rolled down her cheeks and again she buried her face in her hands. Involuntarily he stretched out his hand and stroked her forehead. He felt her whole body tremble as she began to sob, almost inaudibly at first, then gradually louder and finally without restraint. Suddenly she slipped out of the armchair, prostrated herself at his feet, flung her arms around his knees and pressed her face against them. Then she looked up at him with wide open, agonized wild eyes and whispered fervently: "I don't want to leave here. Even if you never came again, and I were never to see you any more; I want to live close by you."

He was more moved than astonished; for he had always known that she was in love with him, or imagined that she was.

"Please get up, Marianne," he said softly as he bent down and raised her gently, at the same time thinking: there's a touch of hysteria involved here too, of course. He gave a sidelong glance at her dead father. Supposing he can hear everything, he thought. Suppose he's in a cataleptic trance? Perhaps everyone is only apparently dead for those first few hours after passing on—? He held Marianne in his arms but a little apart, and feeling a little ridiculous he reluctantly pressed a kiss upon her forehead. Fleetingly he recalled a novel he had once read, in which a very young man, almost a boy, had been seduced, or rather raped at his mother's death-bed by her best friend. In the same instant, he could not for some reason help thinking of his wife. Bitterness against her welled up inside him, and a sullen resentment of the man with the yellow suitcase on the hotel stairs in Denmark. He drew Marianne closer to him, but without feeling in the least aroused; indeed the sight of her lustreless dry hair and the sweetish-stale smell of her unaired clothes filled him with a faint revulsion. Then the bell rang and, with a sense of being released, he hastily kissed Marianne's hand, as if in gratitude, and went to open the door. Dr Roediger was standing outside in a dark gray overcoat and galoshes, with an umbrella in his hand and an earnest expression befitting the occasion on his face. The two gentlemen nodded to one another with greater familiarity than was warranted by their actual relationship. Then they entered the room together and Roediger, with an awkward glance at the dead man, extended his sympathies to

Marianne; Fridolin went into the next room to see to the medical obituary notice, and as he turned up the gas flame above the desk, his gaze fell on the picture of an officer in white uniform, charging with sabre drawn down a hill towards an unseen enemy. It was mounted in a narrow gilt frame and the effect was no more impressive than a modest lithograph.

Fridolin returned with the completed death certificate to the room where the bridal couple were sitting at the father's bedside holding hands.

Again the doorbell rang: Dr Roediger got up and went to open it; meanwhile Marianne, her eyes on the floor, said almost inaudibly: "I love you." Fridolin's only response was to murmur Marianne's name, not without tenderness. Roediger returned with an older married couple. It was Marianne's uncle and aunt; a few appropriate words were exchanged with the usual awkwardness that the presence of someone recently deceased tends to generate. The little room suddenly seemed to be full of mourning guests, and feeling himself no longer needed, Fridolin paid his respects and was conducted to the door by Roediger, who felt obliged to say a few words of thanks and expressed the hope that they might meet again before too long.

III

Outside the door to the apartment block, Fridolin looked up at the window he himself had opened earlier; the frames were quivering slightly in the wind that gave a foretaste of spring. The people who had remained behind up there, the living no less than the dead, seemed equally ghostly and unreal to him. He felt as if he had escaped, not so much from an experience as from some melancholy enchantment that must not gain power over him. The only after-effect he felt was a remarkable reluctance to go home. The snow in the streets had melted, here and there little piles of dirty white snow had accumulated, the gas flames in the street-lamps flickered, and a neighbouring church clock struck eleven. Fridolin decided to spend another half hour in a quiet corner of a coffee-house near his apartment before going to bed and took the route through the Rathauspark. On shadowy benches here and there couples huddled close to one another, as if spring really had arrived and the treacherous warm air were not pregnant with dangers. Stretched out full length on one of the benches lay a ragged-looking man, his hat pressed down over his brow. What if I were to wake him, thought Fridolin, and give him money for a night's lodging? But what good would that do, he went on to reflect, I'd then have to provide for him tomorrow too, otherwise

there would be no point, and perhaps I would be suspected of some criminal association with him. And so
he quickened his pace, as if to escape all forms of responsibility and temptation as fast as possible. Why
him specifically? he asked himself, in Vienna alone
there are thousands of such miserable souls. Supposing one were to start worrying about all of them,—
about the fates of all those unknown people! The dead
man he had just left came into his mind, and with a
shudder of revulsion he reflected how, in compliance
with eternal laws, corruption and decay had already
set to work in that emaciated body stretched out full
length under the brown flannel coverlet. He was glad
that he was still alive, that for him such ugly matters
were still probably a long way off; glad that he was in
his prime, that a charming and lovable woman was
there at his disposal, and that he could have another
one, many others, if he so desired. Such things might
admittedly require more courage than he could mus-
ter; and he reflected that by eight o'clock tomorrow
he would be back at the clinic, that he would have to
visit his private patients from eleven to one, and hold
a seminar from three to five in the afternoon, and that
in the evening too he would be faced with a few further house-calls.—Well, with luck at least he would
not be summoned in the middle of the night again, as
had happened today.

He crossed the Rathausplatz, which glistened
faintly like a brownish pond, and turned towards
home in the Josefstadt district. In the distance he
could hear the regular muffled sound of marching,

and still some way off, just rounding a street corner, he saw a small troop of some six or eight fraternity students coming towards him. As the youths emerged into the light of a street-lamp, he recognised that they were Alemannians from the blue colours they were sporting. He himself had never belonged to a fraternity, but he had taken part in a few fencing-matches in his time. And the memory of his student days put him in mind of the dominoes in red, who had enticed him into their box the night before and contemptuously abandoned him again so soon. The students were now quite close and were laughing and talking loudly;—did he know any of them from the hospital? But in the uncertain light it was impossible to make out their features clearly. He was obliged to stay very close to the wall to avoid colliding with them;—now they were past; but the last one to pass him, a lanky fellow in an open winter overcoat and with a bandage over his left eye, seemed quite deliberately to hold back a little, and thrusting his elbow sideways bumped against him. It could not have been an accident. What does the fellow think he's doing? thought Fridolin, and involuntarily stopped short; after a couple of steps the student did the same, and so for a moment they eyed one another at close range.

But then Fridolin suddenly turned round again and continued on his way. He heard a short laugh behind him,—and was on the point of turning back again to challenge the fellow, but felt his heart beating wildly—exactly as it had twelve or fourteen years ago when there had been a loud knocking at his door while he had been entertaining a charming young lady given to rambling on about a—probably non-existent—bridegroom living some way away; though as it turned out it had only been the postman who had been knocking in so threatening a manner.—And now he again felt his heart racing, exctly as on that occasion. What's all this? he said to himself peevishly, noticing that his knees too were trembling a little. Cowardice—? Nonsense! Am I, a man of thirty-five, a practising physician, married and father of a child, really expected to go challenging some drunken student! Challenges! Witnesses! A duel! And perhaps an arm-wound into the bargain, all because of a stupid incident like that. And then be professionally incapacitated for a few weeks?—Or lose an eye?—Or even blood-poisoning—? Within a week he could well be as far gone as the gentleman under the brown flannel bed-cover in the Schreivogelgasse! Cowardice—? He had fought in three student fencing-matches, and once had even been prepared to duel with pistols, and it certainly was not on *his* initiative that the matter had then been amicably settled. And what about his profession! Dangers on all sides and at every moment,—it was just that one tended to forget about them. How long ago was it that that child with diphtheria had coughed in his face? No more than three or four days. Now that was a far more serious matter than some footling sword-play, and he had not thought twice about it. Well, if he met the fellow again, the matter could yet be resolved. He was scarcely obligated, at midnight on the way to or from a patient—and after all that might have been the case—to respond to the absurd affrontery of some student. Now if on the other hand he were to come across the young Dane, with whom Albertine—no, no, what was he thinking of? But then—it really was no different to her having been his mistress. Worse even. If only *he* were to come towards him now. What a pleasure it would be to stand opposite him in some forest clearing, and aim the barrel of his pistol at that forehead with the fair hair combed across it.

Suddenly he found himself well beyond his intended destination in a narrow street where only a few wretched whores were strolling on their nightly man-hunt. Like ghosts, he thought. And in his memory the students too, with their blue caps, suddenly seemed ghost-like, as did Marianne with her fiancé, uncle and aunt, whom he now imagined sitting hand in hand around the old Court Counsellor's death-bed; Albertine too, who floated before his mind's eye as she might appear when in deep sleep, her arms tucked beneath her neck—even his child, who lay curled up in her narrow white brass bed, and the rosy-cheeked maid with the mole on her left temple,—to him they had all withdrawn into the realm of ghosts. And although this made him shudder a little, there was also something soothing about this feeling, which seemed to release him from all responsibility, indeed from all connection with humanity.

One of the strolling girls was on the point of propositioning him. She was a pretty creature, still quite young but very pale with lips painted red. This could also end in death, he thought, only not *quite* so quickly! *Cowardice* again? Basically, yes. He heard her steps and then her voice behind him. "Won't you come with me, doctor?"

Involuntarily he turned around. "How do you know me?" he asked.

"I don't know you," she said, "but in this district everyone's a doctor."

He had not had anything to do with women of her kind since his high school days. If he were suddenly transported back to his boyhood, would this creature have attracted him? He remembered a passing acquaintance, an elegant young man who was reputed to be a great womanizer, with whom as a student he had once visited a nightclub after a ball, and how as he departed with one of the professional hostesses he answered Fridolin's bewildered look by saying: "It's always the most pleasurable way;—besides, they are not the worst women in the world."

"What's your name?" asked Fridolin.

"Mizzi, of course, what else?"

She had already turned the key in the door to the apartment block, and stepping into the entrance-hall she waited for Fridolin to follow her.

"Hurry up!" she said as he hesitated. Suddenly he was standing next to her, the door fell to behind him, and having locked it she lit a candle and went on ahead to light the way.—Am I mad? he asked himself. I won't touch her, of course.

An oil lamp was burning in the room. She turned the wick up: it was quite a comfortable room, well maintained, and at least it smelled more agreeable than Marianne's quarters, for instance. Admittedly, there had not been an old man lying here sick for months. The girl smiled and without being importunate moved closer to Fridolin, who gently evaded her. Then she pointed to a rocking-chair, which he settled into readily.

"You must be very tired," she said. He nodded. And undressing without haste she went on:

"Ah well, a man like you, with all the things you have to see to all day long. In that respect people like us have it easier."

He noticed that her lips were not made up but were a natural red, and complimented her on them.

"But why should I use make-up?" she asked. "How old do you think I am?"

"Twenty?" Fridolin guessed.

"Seventeen," she said, and seated herself on his lap, throwing her arm round his neck like a child.

Who in the world would guess, he thought, that right now I'm here in a room like this of all places? Would I myself have believed it possible an hour, or even ten minutes ago? And—what for? Whatever for? She sought his lips with hers, but he drew back, and she looked at him with large, rather sad eyes and slipped down off his lap. He almost felt regret, as there had been a comforting tenderness in her embrace.

She picked up a red dressing-gown lying over the back of the ready-made-up bed, slipped into it and crossed her arms over her breasts so that her figure was entirely hidden.

"Is that better?" she asked without mockery, almost shyly, as if she were trying to understand him. He hardly knew what to reply.

"You have guessed right," he said then, "I am really tired, and I find it very pleasant just sitting here in the rocking-chair and listening to you. You have such a sweet voice. Go on, talk to me, tell me something."

She sat down on the bed and shook her head.

"You are afraid," she said quietly,—and then, almost inaudibly, gazing straight ahead, "what a pity!"

These last words sent a warm current surging through his blood. He went over to her and attempted to embrace her, reassuring her that she inspired complete confidence in him, and indeed this was no more than the truth. He drew her to him and started to make love to her as he might to an ordinary girl or a woman that he loved. She resisted, and feeling ashamed he eventually desisted.

Then she said: "One never knows, sooner or later it is bound to happen. You are quite right to be afraid. And if anything were to happen, you would curse me."

She refused the banknote he offered her so resolutely that he did not press her further. She wrapped a narrow blue shawl around her, lit a candle to light the way for him, and accompanied him downstairs to unlock the door. "I'm going to stay at home tonight," she said. Involuntarily he took her hand and kissed it.

She looked up at him atonished, almost frightened, then gave an embarrassed happy laugh. "Just like a proper lady," she said.

The door fell shut behind him, and Fridolin, with a quick glance, memorized the house number so that he could send wine and make up to the poor creature the following day.

IV

In the interim it had become even warmer. A gentle breeze brought the scent of watery meadows and spring in the distant mountains down into the narrow street. Where to now? thought Fridolin, as though it were not at all self-evident that he should at last go home and sleep. Somehow he could not make up his mind to do so. Strange how homeless, how rejected he felt since that disagreeable encounter with the Alemannic students . . . Or was it since Marianne's confession?—No, earlier still—indeed, ever since his evening conversation with Albertine he had been moving away from the habitual sphere of his existence, into some other remote and unfamiliar world.

He wandered up and down the nocturnal streets letting the light foehn wind play across his brows, until at last, with a resolute stride, as though he had reached a long-sought goal, he entered a modest coffee-house, cosy in an old Viennese way, not particularly spacious, moderately lit and little frequented at that hour.

In a corner three gentlemen were playing cards; a waiter who until then had been watching them helped Fridolin out of his fur coat, took his order and laid magazines and evening papers before him on the table. With a feeling of comfort and security, Fridolin began to leaf through the papers. Here and there an item caught his eye. In some Bohemian town German-language street-signs had been torn down. In Constantinople there was a conference on railway-building schemes in Asia Minor, in which Lord Cranford was also taking part. The firm of Benies & Weingruber had gone bankrupt. A prostitute named Anna Tiger had doused her friend Hermine Drobitzky with vitriolic acid in a fit of jealousy. That evening a herring junket would take place in the Sophia Rooms. A young woman, one Maria B. of 28 Schönbrunner Hauptstrasse, had poisoned herself with sublimate.— Somehow all these sad or trivial events had a calming and sobering effect on Fridolin in their dry everyday ordinariness. He felt sorry for the young Maria B.: sublimate, how stupid! At that very moment, while he was sitting comfortably in the café, and Albertine sleeping peacefully with her arms tucked behind her neck, and the Court Counsellor was beyond all earthly cares, Maria B. of 28 Schönbrunner Hauptstrasse was writhing senselessly in agony.

He looked up from the paper and became conscious of someone eying him from the table opposite. Nightingale—? Could it be? The other man had already recognized him, and raising both arms in a gesture of agreeable surprise came over to him—a large, broad, almost burly fellow, youngish still, with long wavy fair hair already streaked with grey, and a drooping moustache after the Polish fashion. He wore an open grey coat over a slightly greasy evening suit, a creased shirt with three synthetic diamond buttons, a crumpled collar and a flapping white silk tie. His eye-lids were red from many sleepless nights but his blue eyes gleamed merrily.

"So you're in Vienna?" cried Fridolin.

"You didn't know," said Nightingale in a soft Polish accent with a slight Jewish intonation. "How come you didn't know? Considering how famous I am." He laughed aloud good-humouredly and sat down opposite Fridolin.

"How have you managed that?" asked Fridolin. "Perhaps you've become Professor of Surgery on the quiet?"

Nightingale laughed even more heartily. "Didn't you hear me just now?"

"How do you mean, hear you?—Ah, I see!" And for the first time Fridolin became conscious of the fact that, as he had entered, indeed even earlier as he had approached the coffee-house, he had heard a piano playing from somewhere in the depths of the establishment. "So that was you?" he exclaimed.

"Who else?" laughed Nightingale.

Fridolin nodded. Yes, of course;—that peculiarly energetic touch, those strange, somewhat haphazard yet melodious chords with the left hand had immediately seemed so familiar to him. "So you've devoted yourself entirely to music?" he enquired. He recalled that Nightingale had finally given up medicine after the second preliminary examination in zoology, which he had passed successfully but only after seven years. Yet he had continued for some time to hang about the hospital's dissecting room, laboratories and lecture halls, where with his artist's shock of fair hair, his invariably crumpled collar, his fluttering once-white tie, he had been a striking, in a light-hearted sense popular, and even perhaps a beloved figure, not only among his peers but with some of the professors. The son of a Jewish dram-shop owner in some Polish backwater, he had in due course reached Vienna from his home town to study medicine. From the outset the allowance from his parents had been negligible, and in any case it soon had been revoked, but this did not prevent him continuing to appear at the get-togethers of one of the medical associations in the Riedhof to which Fridolin too belonged. Payment of his dues had at some stage been taken over in turn by one or other of his more affluent colleagues. Sometimes he was also offered gifts of clothing, which he accepted willingly and with no false pride. He had already learned the rudiments of piano playing in his home town from a pianist stranded there, and while a medical student in Vienna he simultaneously attended the Conservatory, where apparently he was regarded as a talented and promising pianist. But here too he was not serious or industrious enough to develop his gifts systematically; and he soon contented himself with musical success only in his own immediate circle of acquaintances, or rather with the pleasure his piano playing gave them.

For a time he was engaged as pianist in a suburban dancing-school. Fellow students from the university and medical fraternity tried to introduce him to the better houses in the same capacity, but on such occasions he would only play what he wanted and as long as he wanted, he would engage young ladies in conversations which were not on his part always innocently pursued, and would drink more than he could hold. On one occasion he played at a dance in the house of a bank-manager. Well before midnight, having embarrassed the young girls and offended their consorts with his risqué gallantries as they danced past, he took it into his head to play a wild cancan while singing couplets full of innuendoes in his powerful bass voice. The bank-manager rebuked him strongly. In rapturous high spirits, Nightingale got up and embraced the manager who was so appalled that, though himself a Jew, he hissed a Jewish imprecation in his face, to which Nightingale promptly responded by boxing him soundly over the ears—and with this his career in the better houses of the city seemed to close forever. In more intimate circles he generally managed to behave more decently, though even on such occasions he would sometimes in the small hours have to be forcibly removed from the premises. Yet the next morning such incidents were forgiven and forgotten by those involved.—One day, long after his contemporaries had completed their studies, he

had suddenly left town without taking leave of anyone. For a few months greetings cards from him continued to arrive from various towns in Russia and
Poland; and once, without further explanation, Fridolin, of whom Nightingale had always been particularly fond, was reminded of his existence not merely
by a greeting but by a request for a moderate sum of
money. Fridolin sent the money off at once, but never
received any thanks or further sign of life from Nightingale.

And now, at quarter to one in the morning eight
years later, Nightingale insisted on making good this
oversight, and proceeded to take precisely the right
number of banknotes from a wallet which, though
somewhat the worse for wear, appeared tolerably
well-lined, so that Fridolin felt able to accept the re-
payment in good conscience . . .

"You appear to be doing all right," he observed
smiling, as if to put his own mind at rest.

"Can't complain," replied Nightingale. And then
laying his hand on Fridolin's arm, "But now tell me,
what brings you here in the middle of the night?" Fridolin explained that his presence so late at night was
the result of an urgent need for a cup of coffee after a
nocturnal consultation; he did not say however, without quite knowing why, that he had not found his patient alive. Then he talked in a general way about his
medical activities at the clinic and his private practice, and mentioned that he was happily married, and
the father of a six-year-old girl.

Then Nightingale told his story. As Fridolin had

correctly surmised, he had spent all these years as a pianist in various Polish, Romanian, Serbian and Bulgarian towns and villages, and had a wife and four children living in Lemberg;—here he laughed out loud, as though it were exceptionally amusing to have four children, all in Lemberg and all by one and the same woman. Since last autumn he had again been living in Vienna. The variety theatre that had engaged him had almost at once gone bankrupt, and now he was playing in various different night-clubs as occasion arose, sometimes even in two or three on the same night, like down here for instance in this basement tavern,—hardly an elegant establishment, he observed, more like a bowling-alley really, and as for the clientele . . . "But when one has to provide for a wife and four children in Lemberg"—and he laughed again, not quite as heartily as before. "Sometimes I also do some private work," he added hastily. And as he noticed the smile of recollection on Fridolin's face,—"not with bank-managers and their ilk, no, in all sorts of circles, some of them more fashionable, some open and some secret.

"Secret?"

Nightingale looked straight ahead with a gloomy, knowing expression. "They will be picking me up again shortly."

"What, you're performing again tonight?"

"Yes, these things never start before two o'clock."

"Well, that sounds splendid," said Fridolin.

"Yes and no," laughed Nightingale, but he immediately became serious again.

"Yes and no—?" repeated Fridolin curiously.

"I'm playing at a private house tonight, but don't know whose."

"So you are playing for them for the first time?" asked Fridolin with mounting interest.

"No, for the third time. But it will probably be yet another house."

"I don't understand."

"Neither do I," laughed Nightingale. "You'd better stop asking questions."

"Hm," said Fridolin.

"Oh, you're mistaken. It's not what you think. I've seen quite a lot, things you wouldn't believe in such small towns—especially in Romania,—but one lives and learns. Here however . . ." He drew the yellow curtain back a little, looked out onto the street and as if to himself said: "Not there yet,"—adding by way of explanation to Fridolin, "I mean the coach. I'm always picked up by a coach, and it's a different one each time."

"You make me curious, Nightingale," remarked Fridolin coolly.

"Listen," said Nightingale after some hesitation. "If there's anyone in the world I'd do a favour for— but how would we go about it—," adding suddenly: "Do you have the courage?"

"What a question," said Fridolin in the tone of an insulted fraternity student.

"I didn't mean it like that."

"Well, how do you mean exactly? What's so special about this occasion that requires such courage? What could happen to one anyway?" And he gave a short, contemptuous laugh.

"Nothing could happen to *me*, or at worst this might be my last engagement—but that may be the case anyway." He fell silent and again looked out through the gap in the curtains.

"Well then?"

"How do you mean?" asked Nightingale as if summoned from a dream.

"Tell me more. Now you've started . . . Secret shows? Closed societies? Invited guests?"

"I don't know much about it. Most recently there were thirty people, the first time only sixteen."

"A ball?"

"A ball, of course." He now seemed to regret ever having spoken.

"And you provide the music for it?"

"How d'you mean: for it? I don't know what it's for. I really don't. I simply keep on playing—but with my eyes blindfolded."

"Come, now, Nightingale, what sort of song is this you're singing me!"

Nightingale sighed softly. "Well, not completely blindfolded, admittedly. Not so that I can't see anything at all. That is, I can see things in the mirror through the black silk scarf tied over my eyes . . ." And again he paused.

"In a word," said Fridolin impatiently and a little scornfully, but feeling strangely excited . . . "Naked females."

"Don't call them females, Fridolin," replied Nightingale in an offended tone, "you've never seen such women."

Fridolin cleared his throat lightly. "And how high is the entrance fee?" he asked casually.

"You mean tickets and all that? Whatever are you thinking of?"

"Well, how does one get admittance then?" asked Fridolin tight-lipped, drumming on the table.

"You have to know the password, and it's different each time."

"And what about today?"

"I don't know it yet. Not until I get it from the coachman."

"Take me with you, Nightingale."

"Impossible. Too dangerous."

"But a moment ago you yourself were prepared to . . . do me 'the favour.' It shouldn't really be impossible."

Nightingale looked him over critically. "The way you are now—you couldn't get in under any circumstances, since both gentlemen and ladies all wear masks. You don't happen to have a mask and so on with you? Hardly likely . . . Well, next time perhaps. I'll think of something." He pricked up his ears and again looked out on to the street through the gap in the curtains, and taking a deep breath said: "There's the coach. Adieu."

Fridolin gripped him firmly by the arm. "I won't let you get out of it like this. You're going to take me with you."

"But . . ."

"Leave everything else to me. I know it's dangerous—perhaps that's exactly what attracts me."

"But I've already told you—without a mask and
costume—"

"There are places one can hire a mask."

"At one in the morning—!"

"Now listen, Nightingale. There is just such an outfitter's on the corner of the Wickenburgstrasse. I pass
the sign several times a day." And in mounting excite-
ment he continued hurriedly: "You wait here for another quarter of an hour, Nightingale, while I try my
luck with them. The owner of the shop may well live
in the same building. If not—well then I'll simply
have to forgo the whole adventure. Let fate decide. In
the same house there's a café, I believe it's called Café
Vindobona. Tell the coachman that you've forgotten
something there, and when you enter—I'll be waiting
near the door—quickly give me the password, and get
back into your cab; if I've managed to procure a costume, I'll take another cab and follow you at once—
the rest must take care of itself. In any case, I'll
shoulder all responsibility for the risk you're taking,
Nightingale, upon my word of honour."

Nightingale had attempted to interrupt Fridolin
several times, but to no avail. Fridolin flung the
money for the bill on to the table, including an overly
generous tip, which seemed to him in keeping with
the tone of the whole evening, and departed. A closed
coach was standing outside, the coachman in a top
hat sitting motionless on the box;—like a hearse,
thought Fridolin. After a few minutes at a gallop he

reached the corner house in question, rang, and inquired of the porter whether Herr Gibiser the costumier lived in the same building, secretly hoping this would prove not to be the case. But Gibiser did in fact live there, on the floor below the outfitter's establishment, nor did the porter seem particularly surprised at the late visit, indeed, being in an affable mood after Fridolin's handsome tip, he remarked that during the Shrovetide Carnival season it was by no means uncommon for people to come by as late as this to rent out costumes. He lit up the stairwell with a candle from below until Fridolin had rung the doorbell on the first floor. Herr Gibiser himself opened up at once, as if he had been waiting behind the door: he was gaunt, beardless and bald, and wore an old-fashioned floral dressing-gown and a tassled Turkish fez, so that he looked like a comic elder in a play. Fridolin made his request, saying that the price was of no consequence, to which Mr Gibiser replied dismissively, "I ask what's owing to me, nothing more."

He led Fridolin up a spiral staircase to the storeroom. There was a pervasive smell of silk, satin, perfume, dust and dry flowers; here and there in the looming darkness red and silvery objects glinted; then suddenly a string of little lights came on between the lockers of a long narrow gallery stretching back into the gloom. To left and right of them costumes of every imaginable kind were hanging; on one side there were knights, squires, peasants, huntsmen, sages, orientals, fools; on the other, maids of honour, courtly ladies, peasant women, chambermaids and queensof-the-night. Appropriate head-gear was on display above the costumes, so that Fridolin felt as though he were walking down an avenue of gallows-birds on the point of asking one another for a dance. Herr Gibiser followed along behind him. "Have you any particular preference, Sir? *Louis Quatorze? Directoire?* Old Germanic?"

"I want a dark monk's habit and a black mask, that's all."

At that moment a sound of glasses clinking came from the end of the gallery. Startled, Fridolin looked at the costumier, as though he owed him an immediate explanation. Gibiser had stopped short, however, and was reaching for some hidden switch—immediately a dazzling light spread to the far end of the gallery, where a small table decked with plates, glasses and bottles could be seen. Two figures in the red robes of Vehmic Court Judges rose from their chairs to left and right of it, while simultaneously a glittering dainty creature disappeared from sight. Taking long strides, Gibiser rushed towards them, reached across the table and snatched up a white wig, while at the same time a charming young girl, still almost a child, wearing a Pierrette's costume and white silk stockings, wriggled out from under it and came running down the gallery to Fridolin, who was thus obliged to receive her in his arms. Gibiser had dropped the wig on to the table and was holding the two judges on either side of him firmly by their pleated robes. At the same time he called out to Fridolin: "Hold onto the girl for me there, Sir!" The little creature snuggled close to Fridolin, as though seeking his protection. Her narrow little face was powdered white and adorned with several beauty spots, and a scent of roses and powder emanated from her tender breasts;—while her eyes twinkled with mischief and desire.

"Gentlemen," cried Gibiser, "you will remain here until I hand you over to the police."

"What on earth are you thinking of," they both exclaimed. And as if from one mouth: "We were merely responding to an invitation from your little Fräulein."

Gibiser let go of them and Fridolin heard him say: "You will have to give a better account of yourselves than that. Didn't you see straight away that you were dealing with a madwoman?" And turning to Fridolin, "My apologies, Sir, for this little incident."

"Oh, no harm done," said Fridolin. What he would have liked most was to stay on there, or failing that to have taken the girl away with him at once, no matter wherever or whatever the consequences. She gazed up at him enticingly, and yet like a child, as if under his spell. The judges at the end of the gallery were talking animatedly to one another, and Gibiser turned to Fridolin in a business-like manner and asked: "You wanted a cowl, Sir, a pilgrim's hat, a mask?"

"No," said the little Pierrette with shining eyes, "you must give this gentleman an ermine mantle and a red silk jerkin."

"Don't you dare move from my side," said Gibiser, and pointing to a monk's cowl, which was hanging between the costumes of a yeoman and a Venetian senator, observed: "This should be your size, Sir, here's the matching hat, take them quickly, now!"

Here the judges again came forward. "You must let us out at once, Herr Gibisier," they said, to Fridolin's surprise giving the name Gibiser its French pronunciation.

"There can be no question of that," replied the costumier scornfully, "and for the moment you will be so kind as to wait here 'til I return."

Meanwhile Fridolin slipped on the cowl, tying the ends of the trailing white cord into a knot, while Gibiser, standing on a narrow ladder, handed down a black, broad-brimmed pilgrim's hat which Fridolin put on too; yet he did all this as if under compulsion, feeling more and more obliged to stand by the little Pierrette, should any danger threaten her. The mask which Gibiser now handed to him and which he immediately tried on, smelt of an exotic, slightly unpleasant perfume.

"You go on ahead of me," said Gibiser to the young girl, pointing peremptorily toward the stairs. The little Pierrette turned towards the far end of the gallery, and gaily waved a sad farewell. Fridolin followed her gaze and beheld not two Vehmic Court Judges as before, but two slim young gentlemen in white ties and evening dress, though both were still wearing the red masks over their faces. Then Pierrette swung down the spiral staircase, Gibiser went next, and Fridolin followed on behind. In the hall below Gibiser opened the door leading to the inner rooms and said to Pierrette: "Go straight to bed, you depraved young creature! I'll deal with you as soon as I've settled matters with the gentlemen upstairs."

She stood in the door, white and slender, and with a glance at Fridolin sadly shook her head. In a large wall-mirror to the right, Fridolin caught sight of a gaunt-looking pilgrim, none other than himself, and marvelled at how natural all this seemed. The little Pierrette had vanished and the old costumier locked the door behind her. Then he opened the door of the apartment and hurried Fridolin out into the main stairwell.

"Excuse me," said Fridolin, "what do I owe you? . . ."

"Don't worry, Sir, you can pay when you return them; I trust you."

But Fridolin did not move. "Will you give me your word that you will not do the poor child any harm?"

"What business is that of yours, Sir?"

"I heard you refer to the girl as mad before,—and just now you called her a depraved young creature. A remarkable contradiction, would you not agree?"

"Well, Sir," replied Gibiser in a censorious tone, "are not the mad depraved in the eyes of God?"

Fridolin shook himself angrily.

"However that may be," he then observed, "it should be possible to get professional advice. I am a doctor. Tomorrow we'll talk the matter over further."

Gibiser gave a soundless scornful laugh. In the stairwell a light suddenly went on, the door between Gibiser and Fridolin closed and the bolt was immediately thrust home. As he went downstairs Fridolin took off the hat, cowl and mask and put them under his arm, and when the porter opened the door onto the street the hearse with the driver bolt upright on the box was waiting opposite. Nightingale was on the point of leaving the café, and did not seem too pleased that Fridolin was there on time after all.

"So you've really managed to get yourself fitted out?"

"As you see. And the password?"

"So you insist?"

"Absolutely."

"Well then—the password's 'Denmark.' "

"Nightingale, you must be mad!"

"What do you mean, mad?"

"Oh, nothing, nothing. It just so happens that I was on the Danish coast this summer. Well, get in—but take your time, so that I have a chance to pick up a cab over there."

Nightingale nodded and slowly lit a cigarette, while Fridolin rapidly crossed the street, engaged a cab and in a light-hearted tone, as though participating in some prank, directed his coachman to follow the hearse just setting off in front of them.

They drove along the Alserstrasse and then under a railway viaduct out towards the suburbs, passing through ill-lit side-streets with nobody about. Fridolin considered the possibility that his driver might lose track of the coach ahead; but whenever he stuck his head out of the window into the unnaturally warm air, he could still see the other coach a little distance in front, and the coachman in his tall black top hat sitting motionless on the box. It could all end disastrously, thought Fridolin. Yet he was still conscious of the scent of roses and powder that had emanated from the little Pierrette's breasts. What strange adventure did I brush past there? he asked himself. Perhaps I should not have left, perhaps it was my duty not to. Where am I now, I wonder?

They were climbing steadily past modest villas. Fridolin thought he could now make out where they were; years ago he had sometimes found his way up here on walks: this, surely, was the Galitzinberg that they were climbing. Far down to the left, floating in the haze, he could see the city gleaming with a thousand lights. Then, hearing the sound of wheels behind them, he looked back out of the window. Two coaches were following them, and that pleased him since now the driver of the hearse could not possibly suspect him.

Suddenly, with a violent jolt, the coach turned off into a side-road, and they went hurtling down between fences, walls and ridges as if into a ravine. It occurred to Fridolin that it was high time he disguised himself. He took off his fur coat and slipped on the cowl, exactly as he would slip into the sleeves of his linen coat each morning in the hospital; and as though this might somehow redeem him he reflected that, if all went well, in a few hours he would be going about between his patients' beds as he did every morning—a doctor ready to be of service.

The coach came to a halt. Supposing, thought Fridolin, I were to not get out at all now—and drive back at once instead? But where to? To the little Pierrette? Or to the little trollop in the Buchfeldgasse? Or to Marianne, the daughter of the dead Counsellor? Or home? And with a slight shudder he realized that there was nowhere he wanted to go less. Or was it because that path seemed more circuitous to him? No, I can't go back, he thought to himself. My way lies forwards, even were it to my death. He couldn't help laughing at those melodramatic notions, but even so he did not feel altogether at his ease.

There was a garden gate standing wide open. The hearse in front of him drove on further down into the ravine, or, as it seemed to him, into the dark abyss. Evidently Nightingale had already alighted. Fridolin hastily climbed out of his carriage and instructed the coachman to wait at the corner for his return, however long that might be. And to secure his further services, he paid him handsomely in advance, promising him an equal fee for the return ride. The coaches that had followed his drew up, and from the first of these Fridolin glimpsed a veiled female figure getting out. Lowering his mask, he went into the garden, where a narrow path illuminated from the house led to the front door: its two wings sprang open and Fridolin found himself in a narrow white hallway. The sound of a harmonium reached his ears, and on either hand two servants in dark livery were standing, their faces hidden behind gray masks.

"The password?" they whispered in chorus, and he answered: "Denmark." One of the servants took charge of his fur coat and disappeared with it into an

adjacent room, the other opened a door and Fridolin
entered a dark, dimly lit, high-ceilinged room, draped
with black silk hangings. Some sixteen to twenty
masked revellers, all dressed in the ecclesiastical ap-
parel of either monks or nuns, were strolling up and
down. The softly resonant tones of the harmonium,
playing an old Italian sacred tune, seemed to descend
as if from on high. In one corner of the room stood a
small group of people, three nuns and two monks,
who had been looking round at him rather pointedly
and then quickly turning away. Noticing that he was
the only one with his head still covered, Fridolin took
off his pilgrim's hat and strolled up and down looking
as innocent as possible; a monk touched him on the
arm and nodded a greeting, but for just a second his
gaze bored deep into Fridolin's eyes from behind his
mask. A strange sultry fragrance enveloped him, as if
from southern gardens. Again someone touched him
on the arm. This time it was a nun. She too like the
others had covered her brow, head and neck with a
black veil, and her blood-red mouth glistened beneath
her black lace mask. Where am I? thought Fridolin.
Among madmen? Among conspirators? Have I strayed
into a gathering of some religious sect? Had Nightingale perhaps been ordered, or paid to bring someone
uninitiated for them to have a bit of fun with? Yet for
a prank at a masked ball it all seemed far too earnest,
too monotonous and too eerie. A female voice now accompanied the sound of the harmonium, and an old
Italian religious canticle resounded through the room.
Everyone stood still and seemed to be listening, and

Fridolin too surrendered for a while to the marvellous swelling melody. Suddenly a female voice behind him whispered: "Don't turn round. There's still time for you to leave. You don't belong here. If they were to discover you, you would be in serious trouble."

Fridolin started. For an instant he considered heeding the warning. But curiosity, temptation, and above all his pride were stronger than all other considerations. Well, now I've come this far, he thought, let things take what course they will. And without turning round he shook his head in flat refusal.

Then the voice behind him whispered: "Well, for your sake, I'm sorry."

At this point he turned round. He could clearly make out the blood-red mouth gleaming behind the lace veil, and dark eyes sinking into his. "I'm staying," he said in a heroic voice he did not recognize as his own, and turned away again. The singing was rising to a splendid climax, but quite different sounds were now issuing from the harmonium, not at all in the religious mode, but worldly, sensuous and booming like an organ; and looking around Fridolin noticed that all the nuns had disappeared and only monks were left in the room. Meanwhile the voice of the singer too had modulated from gloomy solemnity via an artfully ascending trill into a mood of levity and jubilation. In place of the harmonium a piano had struck up a more impudent and earthy note, and Fridolin immediately recognized Nightingale's wild and rousing touch, while the female voice, hitherto so noble, culminated in a shrill, lascivious screech which seemed to take off through the roof into infinity. Doors on either side had opened, and through one set Fridolin recognized the shadowy outline of Nightingale's figure at the piano, while the room opposite was suffused with dazzling light, and there the ladies were standing motionless, each with a dark veil covering her head, brow and neck, and a black lace mask over her face, but otherwise completely naked. Fridolin's eyes roved hungrily from sensuous to slender figures, and from budding figures to figures in glorious full bloom;—and the fact that each of these naked beauties still remained a mystery, and that from behind the masks large eyes as unfathomable as riddles sparkled at him, transformed his indescribably strong urge to watch into an almost intolerable torment of desire. The other men were evidently experiencing much the same as he was. The first moments of breath-taking delight gave way to sighs of deep distress; a cry escaped from someone; and then suddenly, as if they were being chased, they all charged, now no longer in their monkish cowls but dressed in festive white, yellow, blue or crimson courtiers' clothes, out of the dimly-lit room towards the women, where they were received with insane, almost sinister laughter. Fridolin was the only one left behind still dressed as a monk, and slunk off a little apprehensively into a remote corner, where he found himself close to Nightingale, who had his back to him. Fridolin could see that Nightingale had been blindfolded, but he also thought he noticed that beneath the cloth his eyes were riveted to the tall mirror opposite, where the gaudy courtiers and their naked dancing-partners could be seen reflected.

Suddenly one of the women was standing next to Fridolin and whispered—for no one spoke a word aloud, as though their voices too must remain a secret—: "Why so lonely? Won't you join the dance?"

Fridolin noticed that two noblemen were eyeing him sharply from the other corner, and suspected that the creature at his side—she was slim of build and boyish—had been sent to him to test him and entice him. Despite this he extended his arms towards her and was about to draw her to him, when one of the other women disengaged herself from her dancing-partner and came running over towards Fridolin. He realized at once that it was the person who had warned him earlier. She pretended she had just caught sight of him for the first time, and whispered, though sufficiently distinctly for them to have heard her in the other corner: "So you're back at last?" And laughing gaily: "It's no use, you've been recognized." And turning to the boyish woman: "Leave him to me for just two minutes. Then you can have him again, until morning if you wish." And then more softly to her, and as if elated: "It's him, yes him." The other woman expressed surprise: "Really?" and glided off to join the courtiers in the other corner.

"Don't ask questions," said the one who had remained behind with Fridolin, "and don't be surprised at anything. I have done my best to mislead her, but I can tell you now: it won't succeed for long. Fly while there is time. Any minute it could simply be too late.

Make sure, too, that they don't follow your tracks. No one must discover who you are. It would be the end of your tranquillity, of your peace of mind, for ever. Go!"

"Will I see you again?"

"Impossible."

"Then I'm staying."

A shudder went through her naked body, transmitting itself to him and almost depriving him of his senses.

"No more than my life can be at stake," he said, "and to me at this moment you are worth it." He seized her hands and tried to draw her to him.

Again as if in despair she whispered: "Go!"

He laughed and could hear himself as one hears oneself in dreams. "I know exactly where I am. You are not here, all of you, simply to arouse one by your appearance. You are deliberately playing games with me, so as to drive me completely mad."

"It will be too late, go!"

But he refused to listen to her. "Are there no discreet apartments here, where couples who have discovered one another can retire? Are all those assembled here going to take leave of their partners with a polite kiss of the hand? It doesn't look like it."

And he pointed to the reflection in the mirror of the brilliantly lit adjacent room, where the couples were dancing to the frantic strains of the piano, gleaming white bodies pressed against blue, red and yellow silk. He had the feeling that now no one was paying any attention to him and the woman by his side, as they

stood there alone in the middle room in almost total
darkness.

"Your hopes are vain," she whispered. "There are
no apartments here, such as you imagine. You don't
have a minute to spare. Fly!"

"Come with me."

She shook her head violently, as if in desperation.

He laughed again and couldn't recognise his laugh.
"You can't be serious. Have these men and women
come here just to arouse and then to scorn each other?
Who can forbid you to leave with me, if you so wish?"

She took a deep breath and lowered her head.

"Ah, now I understand," he said. "So this is the
punishment you reserve for anyone who slips in unin-
vited. You could scarcely have conceived of a more
cruel one. Release me from it. Have mercy on me. Impose some other penance. Only don't force me to de-
part without you!"

"You are mad. I cannot leave with you, any more
than—with anybody else. And anyone who tried to
follow me would be forfeiting both his life and mine."

Fridolin was intoxicated, not merely by her presence, her fragrant body and burning red lips, nor by
the atmosphere of the room and the aura of lascivious
secrets that surrounded him; he was at once thirsty
and intoxicated by all the adventures of the night,
none of which had led to anything, by his own audac-
ity, and by the sea-change he felt within himself. He
stretched out and touched the veil covering her head,
as though intending to remove it.

She seized his hands. "One night someone did take

it into his head during the dance to strip the veil from one of us. They tore off his mask and drove him out with a whip."

"And—what happened to her?"

"You may have read about a beautiful young girl—it was only a few weeks ago—who took poison the day before her marriage."

He even remembered the name and mentioned it. Hadn't it been a girl from an aristocratic family, engaged to an Italian prince?

She nodded.

Suddenly one of the courtiers was standing beside them, the most resplendent of them all and the only one in white; and with a curt but polite if somewhat imperious bow, he invited the woman with whom Fridolin was speaking to dance. Fridolin had the impression that she hesitated for a moment. But already the man had put his arm round her and was waltzing away with her towards the other couples in the adjacent lighted room.

Now Fridolin found himself alone, and this sudden abandonment descended on him like a frost. He looked around. For the moment no one seemed in the least concerned about him. Perhaps there was still one last chance that he might escape unpunished. What it was that despite this held him spellbound in his corner, invisible and unobserved—whether it was fear of an ignoble and somewhat ridiculous retreat, or the torment of unsatisfied longing for the mysterious woman's body, whose fragrance still caressed him, or the notion that everything he had seen so far might have been meant to test his courage, and that the gorgeous woman would fall to him as his reward—he did not rightly know himself. At all events, it was clear to him that this suspense was no longer tolerable, and that no matter what the danger, he must bring the situation to a head. Whatever he decided, it could scarcely be a matter of life and death. He might be among fools and perhaps even among profligates, but certainly not among criminals and thugs. And the thought occurred to him that he might go over and join them, acknowledge that he was an intruder, and place himself chivalrously at their disposal. This seemed the only possible way to end the night, with an honourable understanding as it were—if, that is, it were to be anything more than a barren, shadowy succession of dreary, lurid and, scurrilous libidinous adventures, none of which had been pursued through to the end. And with a deep breath he prepared himself.

At that very moment however someone beside him whispered: "The password!" A courtier dressed in black had suddenly approached him, and since Fridolin did not answer straight away he asked a second time. "Denmark," replied Fridolin.

"Quite right, Sir, that is the password for the entrance. The password to the house, if you wouldn't mind?"

Fridolin said nothing.

"Would you be so good as to give us the password to the house?" It sounded sharp as a knife. Fridolin shrugged his shoulders. The other man stepped into the middle of the room and raised his hand, where-upon the piano fell silent and the dance came to a halt. Two other courtiers, one in yellow, the other in blue, came up. "The password, sir," they both said at once.

"I have forgotten it," replied Fridolin with a vacant smile, feeling totally at ease.

"That's unfortunate," said the gentleman in yellow, "for it makes no difference here whether you have forgotten the password, or whether you never knew it."

The other male masked revellers crowded in and the doors on either side were closed. Fridolin stood there alone in his monk's cowl, surrounded by lavishly dressed courtiers.

"Take off your mask!" cried several of them at once. Fridolin held his arm up in front of him as if to shield his face. It seemed to him a thousand times worse to stand there as the only one unmasked amid a host of masks, than to suddenly stand naked among those fully dressed. And in a firm voice he said: "If any of you gentlemen should feel his honour stained by my appearance here, I am quite ready to give him satisfaction in the usual way. But I shall remove my mask only on condition, gentlemen, that the rest of you do likewise."

"It is not a question here of satisfaction," said the courtier dressed in red, who had not spoken before, "but of expiation."

"Take off your mask!" repeated someone else with a clear, insolent voice which reminded Fridolin of an officer's peremptory command. "You shall be told what awaits you to your face, not to your mask."

"I will not remove it," said Fridolin even more sharply, "and woe to him who dares lay hands on me."

An arm suddenly snatched at his face, as if to tear off his mask, when all at once a door opened and a woman—Fridolin had no doubt who it was—stood there, in the habit of a nun, just as when he had first seen her. Behind her in the brilliantly lit room however he could see the others, naked with their faces hidden, huddled together, silent, an intimidated group. But the door closed again immediately.

"Release him," said the nun, "I am willing to redeem him."

There was a moment of profound silence, as though something appalling had occurred, then the courtier in black who had first demanded the password from Fridolin turned to the nun and said: "You are aware of what you are taking upon yourself?"

"Yes, I am aware."

Something like a collective gasp went through the room.

"You are free," said the courtier to Fridolin, "leave the house at once, and beware of delving more deeply into secrets you have merely sneaked across the threshold of. Should you attempt to put anyone on our tracks, whether successfully or not—you will be lost."

Fridolin stood motionless. "In what way is—this woman to redeem me?" he asked.

There was no answer. Several arms pointed towards the door, indicating that he should leave at once.

Fridolin shook his head. "You may impose what penalty you like on me, but I will not tolerate another person paying for me."

"You wouldn't alter anything of this woman's fate," the courtier in black now said very softly. "Here, once a pledge has been given, there is no going back."

The nun nodded slowly as if in confirmation. "Go!" she said to Fridolin.

"No," he replied raising his voice. "Life is no longer worth anything to me if I have to leave without you. I don't ask where you come from nor who you might be. What difference can it make to you, unknown gentlemen, whether you play this Carnival comedy through to its conclusion, whether or not it was intended to end seriously? Whoever you may be, gentlemen, each of you leads another existence outside this one. I however am not playing a part, and if I have done so hitherto under duress, I now will cease to do so. I feel that I have found a destiny which has nothing to do with this charade, and I want to tell you my name, to remove my mask and to take all the consequences upon myself."

"Beware!" the nun cried out, "you would destroy yourself without saving me! Go!" And turning to the others: "Here I am, at your disposal—all of you!"

Her dark costume fell away from her as if by magic, so that she stood there in all the radiance of her white body, and taking hold of the veil wound about her brow, head and neck, with a wonderful circular movement she removed it. It sank to the ground, and her dark hair cascaded over her shoulders, breast and hips,—but before Fridolin managed to catch a glimpse of her face, he was seized by irresistibly strong arms, dragged away and thrust towards the door; a moment later he found himself in the hall, the door behind him closed, a masked servant brought him his fur coat and helped him into it, and the front door opened. As if propelled by some invisible force he hurried out, and regaining the street as the light went out behind him, he turned round and saw the house lying there in silence, with not a glimmer of light escaping from the closed windows. All I have to do is remember everything precisely, was his first thought. If I can find the house again, everything else will follow in due course.

The night stretched all around him, but a little further up where his coach was supposed to wait for him a dim reddish light was shining. From the lower end of the street the hearse appeared, as though he had just summoned it. A servant opened the door.

"I have my own coach," said Fridolin. The servant shook his head. "If it has driven away, I shall return to the city on foot."

The servant replied with a gesture which, far from being servile, clearly brooked no opposition. In the gloom, the coachman's top hat seemed to loom absurdly tall. The wind was blowing briskly and violet clouds were racing across the sky. After all his adventures thus far, Fridolin could not delude himself that he had any choice but to get into the carriage, and promptly it moved off.

Fridolin felt determined, whatever the risk, to get to the bottom of the whole affair as soon as it was feasible. His existence, he felt, would no longer make sense if he failed to find the enigmatic woman, who at that same moment was paying the price of his release. What that would entail was all too easy to guess. But what could be her motive in sacrificing herself for him? Sacrifice—? Was she the sort of woman for whom what she was now facing, what she was preparing to submit to, would really constitute a sacrifice? If she was taking part in such gatherings—and today could scarcely be the first occasion, since she was so familiar with their rituals—what could it matter to her whether she submitted to the will of one or all of these courtiers? Could she be anything more than a cheap whore? What else could any of these women be? All whores without a doubt. Even if they all lead a second, so-called bourgeois life alongside this one, it would still for all that be a whore's life. And wasn't everything he had just experienced in all probability an infamous jest they had indulged in at his expense? A jest that had been anticipated, prepared for and perhaps even built into the proceedings, in case an intruder should manage to sneak in? And yet when he thought about that woman who had warned him from the outset, and who was now prepared to ransom him—there had been something about her voice, her bearing, and the nobility of her

naked figure that could not possibly have been inau-
thentic. Or had his, Fridolin's, sudden appearance
brought about some miraculous reformation in her?
After everything he had experienced that night, he
found it impossible—and he was not conscious of any
affectation in the idea—to believe in such a miracle.
But perhaps there are times, or nights, he thought,
when some strange irresistible magic does emanate
from men who under normal circumstances are not
imbued with any particular power over the opposite
sex?

The coach continued to climb, even though in the
normal course of events it should have turned into the
main road long ago. What were they going to do with
him? Where was the coach taking him? Was the comedy perhaps to have a sequel? Of what kind would it
be? Would it have an enlightening resolution? A happy
reunion somewhere else perhaps? A reward for an ini-
tiation honourably endured and acceptance into the
secret society? Undisturbed possession of the gorgeous nun—? The carriage windows were all closed:
Fridolin attempted to look out—but they were
opaque. He tried to open the windows on either side,
but without success; and the glass partition between
him and the coachman's box was just as opaque, just
as firmly sealed. He knocked at the glass pane,
shouted, screamed, but the coach rolled on. He tried
to open first the left- and then the right-hand door but
they simply would not yield, and his redoubled cries
were lost amid the rumbling wheels and the whistling
of the wind. The coach began to jolt as it drove down

hill at an ever faster pace, and Fridolin, seized by anxiety and fear, was on the point of smashing one of the opaque windows when the carriage suddenly came to a halt. Both doors opened at once as though mechanically operated, now appearing ironically to give Fridolin the choice between alighting either to the right or left. He leaped out of the coach, the doors slammed to,—and without the coachman's paying Fridolin the slightest notice, the carriage drove off through the open fields into the night.

The sky was overcast, the clouds were scudding, the wind whistling, and Fridolin found himself standing in the snow which emitted a faint radiance all about him. And as he stood there with his fur coat open over the monk's habit, the pilgrim's hat on his head, he felt a little eerie. The main highway was a short distance away. A procession of street-lights flickering wanly pointed the direction into town. Fridolin however set out straight ahead, taking a short cut downhill across a fairly steep, snow-covered field, in order to mingle with other people again as rapidly as possible. With soaking feet he reached a narrow, dimly lit street, and continued for a while between high board fences which were creaking in the wind; then rounding the next corner he emerged into a slightly wider street, where modest little houses alternated with vacant lots. A steeple clock struck three. Someone wearing a short jacket was coming towards Fridolin, his hands in his trouser pockets, his head tucked between his shoulders, his hat pressed low over his brow. Fridolin braced himself in readi-

ness for an assault, but to his surprise the tramp did
an about turn and ran off. What was that all about, I
wonder, Fridolin asked himself. Then he remembered
that his appearance must be more than a little uncanny, and taking off his pilgrim's hat he buttoned up
his overcoat, though below it the monk's habit still
flapped about his ankles. Again he turned a corner,
and as he entered the main suburban street, a man
in rural garb approached him and greeted him as one
would a priest. The light from a street lamp fell across
the street sign on the corner house. Liebhartstal,—so,
not very far from the house he had left an hour ago.
For a second he was tempted to take the road back
and await developments nearby the house. But almost
at once he gave up the idea, reflecting that he might
well find himself in serious danger without coming
any nearer to solving the mystery. The thought of the
things that might at that very moment be taking place
inside the villa filled him with horror, despair, shame
and fear. These reflections were so intolerable that
Fridolin almost regretted he had not been set upon by
the tramp, indeed almost regretted he was not lying
against a fence in the back-street with a knife between his ribs. That way this senseless night with its
stupid unresolved adventures might at least have
made some sort of sense. Going home like this, as he
was on the point of doing, seemed to him positively
ridiculous. Yet so far nothing had been lost. Tomorrow
was another day. And he vowed not to rest until he
had again found the beautiful woman, whose dazzling
nakedness had so intoxicated him. Only now did he

think of Albertine,—and even so he felt as though he was obliged to conquer her as well, as though she could not, should not be his again until he had betrayed her with all the others he had met that night, with the naked woman, with Pierrette, with Marianne, and with the little trollop from the narrow backstreet. Shouldn't he also perhaps attempt to track down the insolent student who had barged into him, and challenge him to fight it out with swords, or better still with pistols? What was another man's life to him, indeed, what was his own? Should one always risk it only out of duty or self-sacrifice, never on a whim, or out of passion or simply as a test of fate?

And again it crossed his mind that his body might already be carrying the seed of some fatal disease. Wouldn't it be absurd to die because a child infected with diphtheria had coughed in one's face? Perhaps he was already sick. Didn't he have a fever? Wasn't he perhaps lying at home in bed this very moment,—and hadn't everything he believed he had experienced been nothing more than his delirium?

Fridolin opened his eyes as wide as he could, put his hand to his cheek and brow, and felt his pulse. Scarcely above normal. Everything was fine. He was fully awake.

He continued on down the street towards the city. A few market carts came up behind him and rumbled past, and now and then he passed poorly clad people for whom the day had already begun. Behind a coffeehouse window at a table above which a gas light was flickering, a fat man with a scarf around his neck sat sleeping with his head in his hands. The houses still lay in darkness and only a few isolated windows were lit up. Fridolin was aware of people gradually awakening, and imagined them in bed stretching and preparing to face their sour, miserable day. He too was faced with another day, but not with one that was miserable and dreary. And with a strange quickening of the heart he became agreeably conscious that within a few hours he would be going up and down in his white linen coat between his patients' beds. At the next corner a one-horse cab was waiting, the coachman asleep on the box: Fridolin woke him, gave him his address and climbed in.

V

It was four in the morning as he ascended the stairs to his apartment. The first thing he did was to go into his consulting room and lock the mask and habit carefully away in a cupboard, and as he wanted to avoid waking Albertine he took his shoes and clothes off before entering the bedroom. Carefully he turned up his bedside lamp. Albertine was lying quite still, her arms behind her neck, her half-open lips distressingly contorted by the play of shadows: it was a face unknown to Fridolin. He bent over her brow which puckered at once as if in response to being touched, while her features became curiously distorted; then suddenly she laughed out loud so shrilly in her sleep that Fridolin was startled. Involuntarily he called out to her by name. As if in response, she laughed again in an utterly alien, almost uncanny manner. Fridolin called out to her more loudly. And now slowly and wearily her eyes opened wide, and she looked at him blankly as if she did not recognize him.

"Albertine!" he cried for the third time. Only then did she seem to come to her senses. An expression of revulsion, fear and horror came into her eyes. She raised her arms in a futile and somehow desperate gesture, gaping at him openmouthed.

"What's the matter?" asked Fridolin with bated breath. And as she continued to stare at him in horror, he added soothingly, "Albertine, it's me." She took a deep breath, tried to smile and letting her arms fall back onto the bed-cover, asked in a distant voice, "Is it morning already?"

"Almost," replied Fridolin. "It's past four already. I've just got home." She didn't say anything, so he continued. "The Court Counsellor is dead. He was dying when I got there,—and of course I couldn't— leave the relatives alone at once."

She nodded, yet hardly seemed to have heard or understood him as she stared through him vacantly, and he couldn't help feeling—irrational though the notion seemed to him at once—that she must be aware of what he had been through during the night. He bent over her and stroked her forehead. She shuddered slightly.

"What's the matter?" he asked again.

She just shook her head slowly. He stroked her hair. "Albertine, what's wrong with you?"

"I was dreaming," she said distantly.

"What were you dreaming about?" he asked mildly.

"Ah, so many things. I can't quite remember."

"Perhaps you might be able to."

"It was all so confused—and besides, I'm tired. But you must be tired too?"

"Not in the least, Albertine, and I won't get much sleep now. You know how it is when I get home this late—in fact the sensible thing would be to settle down at my desk at once—it's precisely when it's early in the morning like this that—." He broke off. "But are you sure you wouldn't like to tell me your dream instead?" He smiled a little awkwardly.

"You really should lie down and rest a little," she replied. He hesitated a moment, then did as she wished and stretched out beside her. Yet he avoided touching her. As if there were a sword between us, he thought, remembering how he had made the same sort of half-facetious remark under similar circumstances once before.

They both lapsed into silence and lay there with eyes open, each sensing the other's closeness and remoteness. After a while he rested his head on his arm and gazed at her for some time, as if trying to see more than the mere outline of her face.

"Your dream!" he said again suddenly; and it was as though she had been awaiting this demand. She stretched out her hand towards him; he took it as he was accustomed to, playing with her slender fingers distractedly rather than with tenderness. And so she began:

"Do you remember the room in the little villa on the Wörthersee where I stayed with my parents the summer we became engaged?"

He nodded.

"Well, that's how my dream began, with me entering that room—I don't quite know where from—like an actress coming onto the stage. All I knew was that my parents were travelling and had left me by myself. This seemed strange because the next day was supposed to be our wedding-day. But the wedding-dress had not yet arrived. Or was I perhaps mistaken? I opened the wardrobe to have a look, but in place of the wedding-dress a collection of other clothes was hanging there: resplendent oriental operatic costumes actually. Which should I wear as a wedding-dress? I wondered. Then suddenly the wardrobe closed or disappeared, I don't remember which. The room was brightly lit, but outside the window it was darkest night . . . All of a sudden you were standing out there; galley-slaves had rowed you there, since I could just see them disappearing in the darkness. You were very richly dressed in gold and silk and had a dagger with a silver tassel at your side, and you lifted me out through the window. I too was now splendidly attired, like a princess, and we both stood there under the dawning sky, and a fine grey mist arose about our ankles. It was the district we were so familiar with: there before us lay the lake and mountain scenery, and I could also see the rustic houses like something from a toy-box. We two, however, were hovering, or rather flying above the mist, and I thought to myself: so this must be our honeymoon trip. Soon however we were no longer flying but walking up a forest path, the one leading to the Elizabeth look-out, and suddenly we found ourselves high up in the mountains in a sort of clearing, which was fringed on three sides by woods, while towering up behind was a sheer wall of rock. Above us the starry sky was far bluer and more expansive than in the real world, and formed the ceiling to our bridal-chamber. Lovingly and tenderly, you took me in your arms.

"I hope you loved me just as much," remarked Fridolin smiling wryly to himself.

"Even more so, I suspect," Albertine replied seriously. "And yet, how should I put it—despite our intimate embrace our love was tinged with sadness, as if by a presentiment of suffering to come. All of a sudden it was morning. The meadow was radiant and gaily coloured, the surrounding forest exquisitely bedewed, and sunlight played over the surface of the rock. And we too now felt that it was high time to rejoin the world of everyday society. But now something terrible occurred. Our clothes had disappeared. I was overcome by absolute horror, burning all-consuming shame, and at the same time anger against you, as though you alone were responsible for this misfortune;—and all this horror, shame and anger were infinitely more intense than anything I had ever experienced while awake. You however, fully conscious of your guilt, fled down the mountain naked as you were to find some clothes for us. Once you had disappeared I felt totally at ease. I was neither sorry for you nor worried about you, but simply glad to be alone, and I ran happily across the meadow singing: it was a tune from a dance we had listened to at the masked ball. My voice sounded absolutely wonderful, and I wished that people could hear me far down in the city. I could not see this city, but I somehow knew what it was like. It lay there far below me and was surrounded by a high wall, an utterly fantastic city hard to describe in words. Not exactly oriental, nor yet medieval, but rather first one and then the other, at all events a city that long ago had disappeared forever. But suddenly I was lying stretched out on the meadow in the sunshine,—looking much more beautiful than in real life, and as I lay there a gentleman stepped out of the forest, a young man in a light fashionable suit, looking, I now realize, very like the Dane I told you about yesterday. He continued on, greeting me politely as he passed, but not paying any particular attention to me, and walking straight toward the cliff which he started scrutinizing carefully, as though considering how it might be scaled. At the same time, however, I could see you as well. You were down in the lost city hurrying from house to house, from shop to shop beneath leafy arcades, then through a sort of Turkish bazaar, buying the most gorgeous things that you could find for me: clothes, linen, shoes and jewellery;—and all of this you put into a yellow leather case which seemed to have room for everything. The whole time, though, you were pursued by a motley crowd of people, whom I could not see but only hear their muffled threatening cries. And then the other man appeared again, the Dane who had stopped at the cliff face before. Again he came towards me from the forest,—and I somehow knew that in the interim he had been right around the world. He looked quite different from before, yet was clearly the same person. As on the first occasion he stopped before the cliff, disappeared, then re-emerged out of the forest, disappeared again, and again came back out of the forest; this was repeated two, three or perhaps a hundred times. It was always the same person yet always someone different, and he always greeted me as he came past, until finally he stopped short before me and looked searchingly at me. I laughed seductively, more so than ever in my life before, but when he stretched out his arms toward me I wanted to fly yet failed to do so,—and he lay down with me upon the meadow."

She paused. Fridolin's throat was dry, and in the darkness of the room he noticed that Albertine was hiding her face in her hands.

"A curious dream," he said. "Is that how it ended?" And when she said no: "Well then, continue."

"It's not that easy," she began again. "It's almost impossible to express these things in words. Well—to me it was as though I had lived through innumerable days and nights, as though time and place no longer existed, and instead of the peaceful clearing sur-

rounded by the woods and rock where I had been before there was now an extensive flowery plain
stretching in every direction as far as the horizon. I
had long since—how strange such temporal notions
seem!—ceased to be alone in the meadow with that
man. But whether there were three or ten or a thousand couples there beside myself, whether I could see
them, and whether I gave myself to that man only or
to others as well, I could not say. But just as that earlier feeling of horror and shame transcended anything
conceivable in a wakeful state, it would be equally
hard to conceive of anything in normal conscious life
that could equal the freedom, the abandon, the sheer
bliss I experienced in that dream. And yet throughout
all this I never for a moment ceased to be aware of
you. Yes, I could see you being seized, I think by sol-
diers, though there were clerics too among them, and
I somehow knew that you were to be executed. I
knew this without pity, without horror, with complete detachment. They led you out into a sort of cas-
tle courtyard. There you stood, your hands tied
behind your back and naked. And just as I could see
you even though elsewhere, you too could see me together with the man who held me in his arms, and all
the other couples in that unending tide of nakedness
which surged around me, in which I and the man em-
bracing me represented but a single wave. While you
were standing in the courtyard, a young woman
wearing a diadem and a purple gown appeared at a
high arched window between red curtains. It was the
princess of the land. She gazed down at you with a

severe, questioning look. You stood alone while all the others remained aloof, pressed against the walls, and I could hear an ominous, spiteful mumbling and whispering. Then the princess leaned over the parapet. All became quiet and the princess made a sign, bidding you come up to her, and I knew she had decided to pardon you. But you didn't notice her, or didn't want to notice. Suddenly however, still with your hands tied, but wrapped in a black cloak, you were standing opposite her, not in her chamber but somehow hovering in mid air. She was holding a sheet of parchment in her hand,—your death sentence, in which your guilt and the reasons for your being sentenced were recorded. She asked you—I could not hear her words and yet I know—whether you were prepared to become her paramour, in which case your death sentence would be remitted. You shook your head as a sign that you refused. I was not surprised, since all was preordained and the only possible outcome was that, whatever the danger, you would remain true to me unto all eternity. At this the princess shrugged her shoulders and waved into the void, whereupon you suddenly found yourself in an underground vault being chastised with whips, though I was unable to make out the people who were wielding them. The blood flowed from you in streams, and seeing it flow I was aware of my own horror without being surprised by it. Then the princess came up to you. Her hair was unbound and cascaded down her naked body as she held out the diadem toward you with both hands— and I knew she was the girl you had seen one morning naked on the gang plank of a bathing hut, on the beach in Denmark. She did not say a word, but the unspoken implication of her presence, of her silence even, was whether you were willing to become her husband and so prince of the land. When you again declined she vanished suddenly, but I could see at once that they were erecting a cross for you; not in the courtyard below, but on the boundless flowery meadow where I sat reclining in the arms of my lover among all the other couples. I could see you wandering alone and unguarded through old-fashioned streets, and yet I knew that your path was preordained and any escape impossible. Now you were coming up the forest path. I awaited you expectantly but without any overwhelming sympathy. Your body was covered with welts, though they were no longer bleeding. As you climbed higher and higher the path became broader and the forest fell away on either side, until there you stood at the edge of the meadow, still an incredibly vast distance away. Yet you greeted me with smiling eyes, as if to indicate that you had carried out my wishes and were bringing all I needed:—clothes and shoes and jewellery. But I found your conduct utterly ludicrous and pointless, and felt tempted to laugh in your face with scorn—all because, out of fidelity to me, you had turned down the hand of the princess, submitted to torture, and were now staggering up here to undergo a gruesome death. I ran towards you, and you too quickened your pace—I began to levitate and you too started floating through the air; but then suddenly we lost each other and I realized that we had simply flown past one another. I wanted you at least to hear my laughter while they nailed you to the cross.—And so I burst out laughing as loudly and piercingly as I was able. That was the laughter, Fridolin,—with which I woke."

She fell silent and remained completely still. He too did not move or say a word. At that moment anything would have sounded flat, mendacious and cowardly. The further she had progressed with her narrative, the more ridiculous and insignificant his own adventures so far seemed to him, and he swore to pursue them to the end and report them faithfully to her, and so get even with this woman who had revealed herself through her dream for what she really was, faithless, cruel and treacherous, and whom at that moment he thought he hated more profoundly than he had ever loved her.

He now noticed that he was still holding her fingers in his hand and that, despite his determination to hate this woman, he still felt an undiminished though more painful affection for those cool slender fingers that he knew so well; and involuntarily, indeed positively against his will,—he softly pressed his lips to her hand before relinquishing it. . . .

Albertine still did not open her eyes, and Fridolin thought he could see her mouth, her brow, her whole countenance smiling with a joyous, transfigured, innocent expression, and he felt an impulse he himself did not understand, to bend over her and kiss her pallid forehead. But he restrained himself, recognizing that it was only the very understandable fatigue, after the exciting events of the last few hours, that had assumed the guise of sentimental tenderness.

But however matters stood with him at present, whatever decisions he might reach in the next few hours, what he urgently needed at that moment was to escape, at least for a while, into sleep and oblivion. On the night following his mother's death he had been able to fall into a deep and dreamless sleep, and should he not succeed in doing so tonight? So he stretched out beside Albertine who by now appeared to have gone to sleep. As if there were a sword between us, he thought again. And then: we are lying here side by side like mortal enemies.

VI

He was woken at seven o'clock that morning by the gentle knocking of the maid. He cast a quick glance at Albertine. Sometimes, though not always, this knocking would wake her too. Today she slept on tranquilly, all too tranquilly. Fridolin hurriedly got ready. He wanted to see his little daughter before leaving. She was lying peacefully in her white bed, her hands curled into little fists, the way children do. He kissed her forehead. And once again he tiptoed to the door of the bedroom where Albertine was still lying motionless as ever. Then he left, the monk's habit and pilgrim's hat stowed safely in his doctor's bag. He had worked out his programme for the day carefully and even with a touch of pedantry. First on his list was a visit to a lawyer quite close by who was seriously ill. Fridolin examined him thoroughly, found his condition somewhat improved, expressed his satisfaction with genuine pleasure and prescribed a well-tried remedy with the usual admonitions. Then he went directly to the house in the cavernous basement of which Nightingale had played the piano the previous evening. That establishment was still closed, but in the coffee-house upstairs the lady at the till happened to know that Nightingale boarded at a small hotel in Leopoldstadt. A quarter of an hour later Fridolin drew up in front of it. It was a squalid little boarding house. The lobby smelled of unaired beds, bad fat and chicory coffee. An evil-looking porter with piercing red-rimmed eyes, well accustomed to police interrogations, was willing to furnish him with information. Herr Nightingale had driven up at five that morning in the company of two gentlemen who, perhaps deliberately, had made sure they would be virtually unrecognizable by wearing scarves over their faces. While Nightingale had gone up to his room, these gentlemen had paid his rent for the previous four weeks; and when after half an hour he had still not reappeared, one of them had fetched him down personally, whereupon all three had driven to the Northern District Station. Nightingale had appeared to be extremely agitated; indeed—why should one not tell the whole truth to a gentleman who inspired such confidence—he had tried to slip a note to the porter, but the two gentlemen had intervened at

once. Any letters for Herr Nightingale, the two gentlemen had explained, would be collected by someone
authorized to do so. Fridolin took his leave, thankful
that he had his doctor's bag with him as he came out
of the main door: that way people would not take him
for a lodger but for someone there officially. From
Nightingale there was nothing to be gleaned. They
had been very careful and evidently had every reason
for being so.

Next he drove to the costumier's establishment.
Herr Gibiser opened the door himself. "I am returning
the costume I rented," said Fridolin, "and would like
to pay you whatever is owing." Herr Gibiser named a
modest sum, accepted the money, made an entry in a
hefty ledger, and looked up somewhat puzzled from
his desk, as Fridolin made no sign of leaving.

"I am here, furthermore," said Fridolin in the tone
of a prosecuting lawyer, "to have a word with you
about your daughter."

Herr Gibiser's nostrils quivered faintly,—whether
with uneasiness, mockery or irritation was difficult to
tell.

"What do you mean, sir," he asked in a tone which
was equally hard to interpret.

"Yesterday you mentioned," said Fridolin, one
hand resting on the desk with fingers splayed, "that
your daughter was not quite normal mentally. The
circumstances in which we encountered her actually
make this surmise quite clear. And as chance made
me a participant, or at least witness to that extraordi-

nary little scene, I wanted to urge you, Herr Gibiser, to consult a doctor."

Gibiser, twirling an unnaturally long feather quill in his hand, considered Fridolin with an insolent look.

"And might you, sir, be so obliging as to take on her treatment?"

"I would ask you," replied Fridolin sharply but also a little hoarsely, "not to put words into my mouth which I did not utter."

At that moment the door leading to the inner rooms was opened and a young gentleman, his coat open over his evening suit, came out. Fridolin knew at once that it could be none other than one of the Vehmic Court Judges from the previous night. There could be no doubt that he was coming from Pierrette's room. He seemed put out when he caught sight of Fridolin, but controlling himself at once he greeted Gibiser with a swift wave of the hand, then lit a cigarette with the lighter on the desk and left the apartment.

"I see," remarked Fridolin with a sneer of contempt and a bitter taste in his mouth.

"How do you mean, sir?" asked Gibiser completely unruffled.

"So you decided, Herr Gibiser," he said, gazing meaningfully from the apartment door to the one from which the judge had just emerged, "to dispense with informing the police."

"We have come to a different understanding, Doctor," said Gibiser coolly and stood up, as if an audience had been concluded. As Fridolin turned to go, Gibiser opened the door solicitously and said with an impassive face, "If you should need anything again, sir, . . . it would not have to be specifically a monk's habit."

Fridolin slammed the door behind him. Well, that's seen to, he thought, with a feeling of exasperation that even to him seemed out of all proportion. He hurried down the stairs, made for the polyclinic without undue haste, and telephoned home at once to ensure whether any of his patients had sent for him, whether the post had come, and whether there was any other news. The maid had scarcely finished answering when Albertine herself came to the phone and greeted him. She repeated everything the maid had just said, and without any awkwardness told him she had just got up and was about to have breakfast with the child.

"Give her a kiss from me," said Fridolin, "and enjoy your meal."

Her voice had done him good, and precisely for that reason he rang off almost at once. He had wanted to ask what Albertine's plans were for the morning, but what business of his was that? In the depths of his soul he had after all already done with her, however life might go on outwardly. The blonde nurse helped him out of his coat and handed him his white doctor's tunic. As she did so, she smiled at him a little, as she tended to smile at everyone, whether they were interested in her or not.

A few minutes later he was on the ward. The head physician had left word that he had been suddenly called away for consultation, and his colleagues were to do the rounds without him. Fridolin felt almost happy as he went from bed to bed followed by the students, examining patients, writing prescriptions, and consulting professionally with residents and nurses. There were all sorts of new developments. The locksmith Karl Rödel had died during the night. The post-mortem was at five that afternoon. In the women's ward a bed had become vacant, but already had been filled. The woman from bed seventeen had had to be transferred for surgery. Now and then questions to do with personnel were touched on too. The new appointment as director of the clinic was to be decided the day after tomorrow; Hügelmann, who was currently Professor at Marburg, and four years ago had still only been Stellwag's second assistant, had the best chance. A rapid career, thought Fridolin. I shall never be considered for the headship of a department, because I don't have my dissertation in hand. Too late. But how so? One would have to start doing research again, or pick up work already embarked on much more seriously. Private practice did still leave one enough free time.

He asked Dr Fuchstaler to take charge of the rounds, though he had to admit that he would rather have stayed on than drive out to the Galitzinberg. And yet, it had to be done. He did not just owe it to himself to pursue the matter further; and there were many things still to be attended to today. And so, just in case, he decided to entrust Dr Fuchstaler with the evening rounds as well. The young girl with suspected acute bronchitis over in the last bed smiled at him. She was the one who, during a recent examination, had taken the opportunity to press her breast so intimately against his cheek. Fridolin returned her gaze ungraciously and turned away with a frown. They're all the same, he thought bitterly, and Albertine no different from the rest—in fact she's the worst of them all. We will have to part. Things can never be the same again between us.

On the stairs he exchanged a few words with a colleague from the surgical department. Well, how was the woman who had been transferred to them last night coming along? Personally, he didn't see the need to operate. Would they forward the results of the histology tests to him?

"You may depend upon it, my dear colleague."

At the corner he took a cab. He consulted his notebook—an absurd little charade for the coachman's benefit—as though he were just making up his mind. "Ottakring," he said finally, "take the road up the Galitzinberg. I'll tell you where to stop."

In the cab he was again suddenly overwhelmed by an ardent yet anguished feeling, indeed almost a sense of guilt, at having scarcely thought about his beautiful saviour during the last few hours. Would he be able to find the house again? It shouldn't be all that difficult. The question was: what then? notify the police? That could have dangerous consequences for the woman who perhaps had sacrificed herself, or been prepared to sacrifice herself for him. Or should he engage a private detective? That seemed rather sordid and not quite worthy of him. But what else could he do? He had neither the time nor, probably, the talent to carry out the necessary investigations effectively himself.—A secret society? Well, secret undoubtedly. But among themselves, were they personally acquainted? Aristocrats, even attached to the court perhaps? He thought of certain archdukes whom one could imagine capable of this kind of escapade. And the ladies? Probably . . . rounded up from various houses of ill repute. Well, that was far from certain. High-class merchandise, at all events. But what about the woman who had sacrificed herself for him? Sacrificed? Why did he persist in imagining that it had really been a sacrifice! A charade. Quite obviously the whole thing had been a charade. Actually, he should be glad that he had got out of it so lightly. Well, at least he had preserved his dignity. The courtiers must certainly have noticed that he was no greenhorn. She at all events had noticed it. Very probably she preferred him to all those archdukes or whatever they had been.

At the end of the Liebhart valley where the road begins to climb more steeply, he got out, dismissing the cab as a precaution. The pale blue sky was flecked with little white clouds, and the sun was shining with the warmth of spring. He looked back—but could see nothing to arouse suspicion. No cab, no one on foot. Slowly he walked up the hill. His coat began to feel heavy; he took it off and threw it over his shoulder. He reached the spot where he had to turn right into the side-road leading to the mysterious house; he couldn't go wrong; the road descended, but not as steeply as he had imagined when being driven down during the night. A quiet road. In one front garden there were rose-bushes wrapped carefully in straw, while in the next there was a small pram, a little boy clad in blue woollen clothes was tottering to and fro; from a ground-floor window a young woman watched him with a smile. Then came a vacant plot, then a fenced-off garden run to seed, then a small villa, then a stretch of lawn and here, there could be no mistake—, here was the house that he was looking for. It didn't look particularly large or grand, being a modest, single-story Empire-style villa which had evidently been renovated not too long ago. The green shutters were all let down and there was nothing to indicate that the villa was inhabited. Fridolin looked all around. There was no one about in the street, apart from two boys further down who were walking away from him with books under their arms. He stood outside the garden gate. What next? Should he simply walk away? That seemed too ridiculous. He looked around for the bell. And supposing they were to open the door, what should he say? Well, simply enquire, perhaps, whether this fine country residence might be available for rent over the summer? But the front door had already opened and an old servant in simple morning livery came out and walked slowly down the narrow path toward the garden gate. He was holding a letter which he silently handed through the bars to Fridolin, whose heart was pounding.

"For me?" he asked hesitantly. The servant nodded, turned and withdrew and the front door closed behind him. What can this mean? Fridolin asked himself. Perhaps it's from her? Perhaps *she* is the one who owns the house—? He walked quickly back up the street and only then noticed that his name was written on the envelope in imperious gothic lettering. At the corner he opened the letter, unfolded the sheet and read: "Give up your investigations which are completely futile, and consider this a second warning. We hope, for your sake, that a further one will not be necessary." He let the note fall to his side.

This message disappointed him in every way; but at least it was quite different from what he had foolishly imagined. Certainly its tone was rather more restrained than cutting. And it suggested that the people who had sent it did not feel at all secure.

A second warning—? Why? Ah yes, the first had been the one issued to him the previous night. But why a second—and not a final warning? Did they want to try his courage yet again? Did he have to pass some sort of test? And how did they know his name? Well, there was nothing strange about that, they had probably forced Nightingale to reveal it. And besides—involuntarily he smiled at his own forgetfulness—his monogram and full address were sewn into the lining of his coat.

Yet even if he had progressed no further than before—on the whole, the letter had been reassuring—although quite why this should be so he could not say. To be more precise, he was convinced that the woman for whose fate he had feared was still alive, and that he alone could find her if he proceeded with cunning and circumspection.

When he reached home a little tired, yet in a strange mood of release which at the same time he felt to be deceptive, Albertine and the child had already had their lunch, but kept him company while he ate his meal. There, sitting opposite him, was the woman who last night would have calmly had him crucified, now looking angelic, domesticated and maternal, and to his surprise he felt no hatred for her whatsoever. Savouring his food, he found himself in an excitable but also more light-hearted mood, and as was his wont, talked animatedly about the day's little professional incidents, dwelling particularly on matters to do with medical personnel, which he was accustomed to relay to Albertine in detail. He explained that the nomination of Hügelmann was as good as certain, and mentioned his own resolve to resume research more vigorously. Albertine was familiar with these moods, and knew that they tended not to last that long, and a smile betrayed her scepticism. Fridolin became more enthusiastic, and Albertine gently stroked his hair to soothe him. He winced slightly and turned towards the child, thus evading further painful contact. He lifted the child onto his lap, and was beginning to rock her on his knees when the maid announced that several patients were already waiting. As if released, Fridolin stood up, and observing casually that Albertine and the child ought to take advantage of the beautiful sunny afternoon and go out for a walk, he entered his consulting-room.

In the course of the next two hours Fridolin had six regular patients and two new ones to attend to.

During each individual appointment he was in excellent form, examining his patients, making notes, prescribing—and was pleased to find himself feeling so wonderfully fresh and clearheaded after two nights spent almost entirely without sleep.

When he had finished his consulting, as usual he looked in again on his wife and child, and was pleased to see that Albertine's mother had dropped in for a visit, and that the child was having a lesson with her French teacher. And it was not until he reached the stairs that he again had the sense that all this order, balance and security in his life were really an illusion and a lie.

Even though he had excused himself from the afternoon rounds, he found himself irresistibly drawn to the clinic. There were two cases that were particularly relevant to his more immediate research plans, and for a while he occupied himself with them more intensively than he had previously done. Then he had one more call to attend to in the centre of town, so that by the time he found himself outside the old house in the Schreyvogelgasse it was already seven in the evening. Only then, as he looked up at Marianne's window, did her image, which had faded more than that of all the others in the interim, come to life again. Well, here at least he would not go unrequited. Here he could begin his work of vengeance without too much trouble; here there were no difficulties and no danger; and the betrayal of a bridegroom, which might have given others pause, was for him merely an additional inducement. Indeed, the idea of betrayal, lying, infidelity and a bit of hanky-panky here and there, all under the nose of Marianne, Albertine, the good Doctor Roediger, all the world;—the thought of leading a kind of double life, of being at once a hard-working reliable progressive doctor, a decent husband, family man and father, and at the same time a profligate, a seducer and a cynic who played with men and women as his whim dictated—this prospect seemed to him at that moment peculiarly agreeable—and the most agreeable thing of all about it was that later on, when Albertine imagined herself secure in the haven of a tranquil conjugal and family life, he would be able to smile coldly and confess his sins to her, and thus get even for all the bitterness and shame she had brought upon him in her dream.

In the entrance hall he found himself face to face with Dr Roediger, who held out his hand to him with unsuspecting cordiality.

"How is Marianne?" asked Fridolin. "Has she calmed down a little?"

Dr Roediger shrugged his shoulders. "She has been expecting the end long enough, Doctor.—It was only when they collected the body around noon today—."

"Ah, so that's already taken place?"

Dr Roediger nodded. "The funeral is at three o'clock tomorrow afternoon . . ."

Fridolin looked straight ahead. "The relatives—are they still with Marianne?"

"No," replied Dr Roediger "she is alone at present. I'm sure she'll be pleased to see you again. Tomorrow my mother and I are taking her to Mödling," and in response to Fridolin's polite look of enquiry: "You see, my parents have a little house there. Good-bye, doctor. I still have several matters to attend to. The things that have to be seen to in a—case like this! I hope I shall see you again upstairs when I get back. And he stepped out of the door into the street.

Fridolin hesitated a moment, then slowly climbed the stairs. He rang and Marianne herself opened the door. She was dressed in black and she had a black necklace made of jet around her neck, which he had never seen her wear before. Her face gradually turned red.

"You've taken your time coming," she said with a wan smile.

"My apologies, Marianne, but it's been an usually busy day today."

He followed her through the dead man's room where the bed now stood empty into the adjacent room where yesterday he had made out the Councillor's death-certificate beneath the picture of the officer in the white uniform. A little lamp was still burning on the desk, so that a dim light suffused the room. Marianne bade him take a seat on the black leather divan, while she herself sat down on the desk opposite.

"I just met Dr Roediger in the hall.—So you are off to the country tomorrow already?"

Marianne looked at him as though surprised at the cool tone of his question, and her shoulders drooped as he continued in a voice that sounded almost harsh: "I think that's very sensible." And he went on soberly to explain how beneficial the effects of the good air and change of scene would be.

She sat there without moving and tears flowed down her cheeks. He observed this without the slightest compassion, indeed with impatience, and was filled with alarm at the thought that any minute she might perhaps again prostrate herself at his feet and renew her declaration of the day before. And as she said nothing he got up briskly. "I'm very sorry, Marianne, but—" and he looked at his watch.

She raised her head, looked at Fridolin, and her tears continued to flow. He would have liked to offer a few words of comfort, but couldn't bring himself to do so.

"I imagine you will be spending several days in the country," he began awkwardly. "I do hope you will let me know how you . . . Dr Roediger tells me that your wedding is to be quite soon, by the way. Allow me to congratulate you both."

She did not stir, as though she had not registered his congratulations or his farewell. He held out his hand, but she did not take it, and in a tone almost of reproach he repeated, "Well, I sincerely hope you will let me know how you are getting on. Good-bye, Marianne." She just sat there as if turned to stone. He began to leave, pausing at the door for a second as if to give her one last chance to call him back, but she seemed instead to have turned her head away, and so he closed the door behind him. Outside in the passage he felt something bordering on remorse. For a moment he considered turning back, but felt that that would have been even more ridiculous.

But what now? Home again? Where else! After all, he could not embark on anything more today. What about tomorrow? And how should he set about things? He felt helpless and inept and everything seemed to be slipping from his grasp; everything was becoming increasingly unreal, even his home, his wife, his child, his profession, his very identity as he trudged on mechanically through the evening streets, turning things over in his mind.

The town hall clock struck half past seven. But it really did not matter how late it was: time seemed to stretch out before him in utter superfluity. No one and nothing concerned him any longer. He felt full of self-pity. Fleetingly, and without any serious intent, he thought of driving to some station, taking a train to wherever it might be and vanishing from the lives of everyone who knew him, to resurface somewhere overseas and begin a new life as someone else. He remembered a number of remarkable cases of double identity he knew about from books on psychiatry: a person would disappear suddenly from a perfectly orderly milieu, be forgotten, and then return months or years later unable to remember where he had been for all that time; then later someone who had known him in some distant land would recognize him, yet the home-comer would know nothing about it whatsoever. True, such things happened very rarely, but they had been authenticated nonetheless. And in a milder form they were experienced by a great many people.

What about when one awoke from dreams, for example? Of course, there one could remember . . . But there were also surly dreams one forgot completely, of which nothing remained but some mysterious aura, some obscure bemusement. Or else one remembered later, much later, and could no longer tell whether one had experienced something or merely dreamed it. Except that—!

And as he wandered on, unconsciously heading in the direction of his apartment, he found himself not far from the dark, rather disreputable street where less than twenty-four hours ago he had followed that abandoned creature to her tawdry yet comfortable lodgings. But why should she particularly be thought of as *abandoned*? Or this particular street be called *disreputable*? Curious how, seduced by words, again and again one labels and condemns people, destinies and streets through sheer idle force of habit. Hadn't that young girl been the most charming and even the purest of all those with whom the strange circumstances of the previous evening had brought him into contact? He felt himself becoming a little aroused as he thought of her. Then he also recollected his intentions on the previous day and, quickly making up his mind, he went into the next shop to purchase various dainty things to eat; and as he continued on close to the walls of the houses with his little parcel, he felt almost happy at the thought that he was about to do something sensible and even perhaps praiseworthy. Despite this, however, he turned up his collar as he stepped into the entrance hall, and ran up the stairs several steps at a time. The apartment doorbell re-sounded in his ears with an unpleasant shrillness, and when he was informed by an evil-looking woman that Mizzi was not at home, he breathed a sigh of relief. But before the woman had a chance to accept the package for the absent girl, another youngish, not un-attractive woman wrapped in a sort of dressing-gown came out into the hall and said: "Who are you looking for, Sir? Mizzi? She won't be back in a hurry."

The old woman signalled to her to be quiet; but Fridolin, eager to receive confirmation of what he had somehow already surmised, simply said: "She's in hospital, isn't she?"

"Well, if you already know, Sir! But I'm quite healthy, thank God," she protested gaily and came up close to Fridolin with half-open lips, thrusting her op-ulent body back cheekily, so that her dressing-gown came undone. "I just came up as I was passing to give something to Mizzi," said Fridolin evasively, and sud-denly he felt like a schoolboy. Then in an altered, mat-ter-of-fact tone he asked: "Which clinic is she in?"

The young woman mentioned that of a professor under whom Fridolin had been an intern several years ago. Then she added good-naturedly: "Let me have the little parcel, I'll bring it to her tomorrow. You can trust me not to nibble. And I'll be sure to send your greetings and to tell her you've been true to her."

At the same time however she moved closer and smiled at him. But when he drew back a little, she gave up the idea at once and remarked consolingly:

"The doctor said she should be home again in six or eight weeks at the latest!"

When Fridolin stepped out of the main door into the street, he felt tears welling up in his throat; yet he was well aware that this was not so much an indication that he had been moved as a sign of incipient nervous collapse. He deliberately started off at a brisker and more vigorous pace than was appropriate to his state of mind. Was this latest experience to be taken as a further, a final indication that all his efforts were doomed to failure? But how so? His escape from such a serious danger could equally well be taken as a propitious omen. And wasn't avoiding danger precisely what everything depended on? Many more perils were bound to lie ahead. And he had no intention of abandoning his enquiry after the beautiful woman of the previous night. Admittedly time was now running out. And besides, the manner in which this enquiry was to be conducted had to be considered carefully. If only there were someone he could consult! But he did not know anyone he would have been willing to confide in about last night's adventures. For years he had not been on intimate terms with anyone except his wife, and he could hardly consult her on this matter—neither this nor any other matter. For whichever way one wished to look at it, last night she had had him crucified.

And now he understood why instead of taking him home his steps unconsciously kept leading him in the opposite direction. He simply could not face Albertine just yet. The most sensible thing was to have his evening meal out somewhere, then see to his two patients at the hospital—and under no circumstances go home—"home!"—before he could be certain that Albertine would already be asleep.

He entered a coffee-house, one of the quieter, more formal ones near the town hall, telephoned to say that they should not expect him home for supper, hastily rang off lest Albertine should come to the phone, and then took a window seat and drew the curtain. A gentleman inconspicuously dressed in a dark overcoat sat down in a remote corner of the room. Fridolin remembered having seen his features somewhere before during the day. That could of course have been mere coincidence. He picked up an evening paper and read a few lines here and there, as he had done the previous evening in another coffee-house: reports on political events, the theatre, art, literature and all sorts of misadventures, large and small. In some town in America he had never heard of a theatre had burned down. Peter Korand, a master sweep, had thrown himself out of a window. To Fridolin it somehow seemed odd that even chimney-sweeps should commit suicide occasionally, and he couldn't help asking himself whether the man had had a proper wash beforehand, or simply plunged into oblivion all blackened as he was. In a fashionable hotel in the centre of the city a woman had taken poison: a lady who had checked in there a few days before under the name of Baroness D., a lady of quite remarkable beauty . . . Well there were so many remarkably beautiful young ladies . . . There was no reason to assume that Baroness D., or rather the lady who had checked into the hotel under the name of Baroness D., and the person he was thinking of were one and the same. And yet— his heart was pounding and the paper trembling in his hand. In a fashionable hotel in the centre . . . which one—? Why so mysterious?—So discreet? . . .

He put the paper down and noticed the gentleman over in the far corner quickly thrust a large illustrated newspaper in front of his face like a screen. Immediately Fridolin too picked up his paper again, and in that instant he knew for certain that Baroness D. could be none other than the woman of the previous night . . . In a fashionable hotel in the centre of town . . . There weren't all that many that would have been considered acceptable—by a Baroness D. . . . And now, come what may, this lead had to be followed up. He summoned the waiter, paid and left. At the door he turned again towards the suspicious gentleman in the corner. But strangely enough, he had already disappeared . . .

A serious case of poisoning . . . But she was alive . . . At the time they had discovered her, she was still alive. And after all, there was no reason to assume that they had not rescued her in time. In any event, dead or alive, he was going to find her. He was going to see her—come hell or high water—whether she was alive or dead. He simply had to see her; nobody on earth could prevent his seeing the woman who had gone to her death for his sake, indeed *in place of him!* He was to blame for her death—he alone—if she in- deed was. Yes, it was her without a doubt. She had come home at four in the morning in the company of two gentlemen. Probably the same two who had escorted Nightingale to the station a few hours later. They could scarcely have a very clear conscience, either of them.

He stood in the broad open square in front of the town hall and looked around. There were only a few people in sight, and the suspicious gentleman from the coffee-house was not among them. And what if he were—these men were clearly frightened, and he was more than a match for them. Fridolin hurried on and taking a cab from the Ringstrasse drove first to the Hotel Bristol, where as if authorized or commissioned to enquire, he asked the porter whether Baroness D. who was said to have poisoned herself that morning, had been staying at this hotel. The porter did not seem especially surprised, perhaps because he took Fridolin to be someone from the police or some official, at all events he politely replied that the unfortunate event had not occurred here but at the Hotel Archduke Karl . . .

Fridolin drove at once to the hotel in question, and there received the news that Baroness D. had been rushed to the General Hospital as soon as she had been discovered. Fridolin enquired how the suicide attempt had come to light. What had caused them to become concerned at noon about a lady who had not arrived home until four that morning? Well, that was simple enough: two gentlemen (again two gentlemen!) had asked for her at about eleven o'clock. As the lady had not responded to repeated telephone calls, the chambermaid had knocked on her door; and since there was still no response and the door was locked from within, they had had no choice but to break it open, and had found the Baroness lying in bed unconscious.

"And the two gentlemen?" asked Fridolin, feeling like someone from the secret police.

Well yes, one couldn't help wondering about the two gentlemen, since while all this was going on they had disappeared without a trace. Furthermore, they had not apparently been dealing with a real Baroness Dubieski, the name under which the lady had registered at the hotel. This was the first time she had ever stayed at that hotel, and at least among the aristocracy there was no family of that name.

Fridolin thanked him for the information, and as one of the hotel managers who had just come up was beginning to look at him with disconcerting curiosity, he withdrew in some haste, got back into his cab and drove over to the hospital. At the reception desk a few minutes later, he not only learned that the ostensible Baroness Dubieski had been delivered to the second in-patients' clinic, but that despite the best efforts of the doctors, she had died at five that afternoon without regaining consciousness.

Fridolin heaved a sigh of relief, or so he imagined, but it was a heavy sigh that escaped him for all that. The official on duty looked up at him in some surprise. Fridolin pulled himself together at once, took leave of him politely and a minute later was standing in the open air. The hospital garden was almost deserted. In an avenue close by a nurse in a white bonnet and blue-and-white-striped smock was just walking past under a street lamp. "Dead," said Fridolin aloud to himself.—If it's her. What if it isn't? And if she's still alive, how am I to find her?

The question of where the body of the unknown woman was at that moment could be answered readily enough. As she had only died a few hours ago, she would still be in the mortuary, only a few hundred yards from there. And for him as a doctor of course, there would be no difficulty about gaining admission, even at that late hour. And yet—what did he hope to achieve there? After all, he had only seen her body, never her face, except fleetingly last night as he had left the dance-hall, or more accurately, been expelled from it. He had not taken this factor into consideration before, because ever since he had first read the notice in the paper he had been imagining the faceless suicidal woman as having Albertine's features, indeed, as he now realized with a shudder, his wife had been incessantly hovering before his eyes as the woman he was seeking. And again he asked himself what he really hoped for in the mortuary? Were he to have found her alive again, today, tomorrow—years hence, no matter when, where or under what circumstances, he was utterly convinced that he would have recognized her at once from her walk, her bearing, and above all her voice. As it was, however, all he would be seeing again was her body, a dead female body—a face he was unfamiliar with except for the eyes—eyes which were now extinguished.

Yes—he knew those eyes and that hair too, which at the very last minute before they dragged him from the room had been let down to cover her nakedness. Would that be enough for him to tell, without the shadow of a doubt, whether or not it was she?

With slow hesitant steps he made his way across the courtyards to the Pathology Institute. He found the main gate unlocked so that he did not have to ring. The stone floor echoed beneath his feet as he walked along the dimly-lit passage. A familiar, almost domestic smell of various chemicals, which drowned out the native odour of the building, enveloped Fridolin. He knocked at the door of the histology lab, where he suspected there might be a technician still at work. On hearing a rather irritable "Come in," he entered the high-ceilinged, almost festively illuminated room, in the middle of which, as Fridolin had half expected, his old fellow student, the Institute technician Dr Adler had just withdrawn his eye from the microscope, and was now rising from his chair.

"Ah, my dear colleague," said Dr Adler, still a little reluctantly but also with surprise, "to what do I owe the honour at such an unusual hour?"

"Sorry to disturb you," said Fridolin. "You are in the middle of something."

"I am indeed," replied Adler with an acerbity that had been characteristic of him even during their student days. Then he added in a lighter tone: "What else would one be doing in these hallowed halls at midnight? But of course you are not disturbing me in the least. How can I be of service?"

And as Fridolin did not reply at once: "Addison, whom you sent down to us today, is still lying in untouched loveliness over there. Post-mortem tomorrow morning at eight-thirty."

And in response to Fridolin's gesture of demurral: "I see, then it's the lung tumour! Well, the histology test revealed an indisputable sarcoma. So no need to go grey over that one."

Fridolin shook his head again. "It's not a—professional matter."

"Well, so much the better," said Adler, "I was beginning to think a guilty conscience might be driving you down here at this ungodly hour."

"It does in a way have to do with a guilty conscience, or rather with questions of conscience in general."

"Oh!"

"Well, to put it bluntly,"—he endeavoured to find an appropriately dry, innocuous tone—"I wanted some information about a woman who died of morphine poisoning in the second clinic this evening and should by now have been laid out down here, supposedly a certain Baroness Dubieski." And he continued more quickly: "You see, I suspect this Baroness Dubieski may be a person I knew briefly many years ago. And I am curious to know whether my suspicion is correct."

"*Suicidium*?" asked Adler.

Fridolin nodded. "Yes, she killed herself," he said, translating, as if by doing so he could reaffirm the private nature of the whole business.

Adler humorously pointed a finger at Fridolin. "Out of unrequited love for your lordship?"

Fridolin demurred a little irritably. "This Baroness Dubieski's suicide has nothing whatsoever to do with me personally."

"I beg your pardon, I have no wish to be indiscreet. We can go and check at once. To my knowledge, there have been no requests this evening from the forensic people. Well, anyway—."

A legal inquest, flashed through Fridolin's mind. It might well come to that. Who knows whether her suicide was really deliberate? He again thought of the two gentlemen who had disappeared so suddenly from the hotel, after they had learned about the suicide attempt. The whole affair might still turn into a criminal case of the first order. And might not he—Fridolin—be summoned as a witness—indeed, wouldn't he be obligated to report to the law-court of his own free will?

He followed Dr Adler across the hall to the door opposite, which stood ajar. The high, bare room was dimly illuminated by the low flame from a double gas lamp. Only a few of the twelve or fourteen mortuary beds were occupied. One or two corpses were lying there stark naked, the others were covered with a linen sheet. Fridolin went up to the first table, next to the door, and carefully removed the sheet from the head of the deceased. Suddenly it was lit up by the harsh light from Dr Adler's pocket torch. Fridolin saw a yellow, grey-bearded man's face and covered it with the shroud again at once. On the next table lay the thin naked body of a young man. Coming over from another table, Dr Adler said: "A woman in her sixties or seventies, that wouldn't be her."

But Fridolin, as though suddenly and irresistibly drawn there, had moved over to the far end of the room, where he could dimly make out the pale corpse of a woman. The head was lying to one side; long dark strands of hair fell almost to the floor. Involuntarily Fridolin stretched out his hand to adjust the head, but then, with a revulsion normally quite alien to him as a doctor, he hesitated. Dr Adler had come up and gesturing towards those behind them said: "It can't be any of the others—what about her?" And he flashed his torch at the woman's head, which Fridolin, overcoming his aversion, had just taken in both hands and raised a little. An ashen face with half-closed lids stared back at him. The jaw hung open loosely, the thin raised upper lip left the bluish gums and a row of white teeth exposed. Whether this face had ever been beautiful, whether yesterday it had still been so, Fridolin would not have cared to say: now it was a completely null, vacant face, the face of death. It could equally well have belonged to a woman of eighteen or thirty-eight.

"Is this her?" asked Dr Adler.

Unconsciously Fridolin bent lower, as if the intensity of his gaze might wrest an answer from those rigid features. And yet at the same time he was conscious that even if it were *her* face, *her* eyes, the same eyes that yesterday had gazed into his ablaze with life, he could never know for certain—and perhaps

didn't even want to know. Gently he laid the head
back against the slab, and let his gaze follow the
torch-light over the dead body. Was it her body?—that
wonderful, blooming body that yesterday had tor-
tured him with longing? He looked at the yellowish,
wrinkled neck, noticed the two small girlish, yet
slightly sagging breasts, between which the breast-
bone stood out under the pale skin with gruesome
clarity, as if the process of decay already had set in;
followed the contours of her lower body, noticing the
way the well-formed thighs spread out impassively
from shadowy regions that had lost their mystery and
meaning; and observed the slight outward curve of
the knees, the sharp outline of the shinbones and
the slender feet with toes turned inwards. One after
the other these features receded once more into the
gloom, as the beam from the torch swiftly retraced its
path, and, trembling slightly, came to rest on the face
again. Involuntarily, indeed as if driven by some unseen power, Fridolin touched the woman's brow,
cheeks, arms and shoulders with both hands; then he
intertwined his fingers with the dead woman's as if
to fondle them, and, stiff as they were, they seemed
to him to be trying to move and to take hold of his;
indeed he thought he could detect a faint and distant
gleam in the eyes beneath those half-closed lids, trying to make contact with his own; and as if drawn on
by some enchantment he bent down over her.

Then suddenly he heard a whisper close behind
him: "What on earth are you up to?"

Fridolin came abruptly to his senses. He let go the

dead woman's fingers, took hold of her slender wrists and carefully, even a shade pedantically, placed her ice-cold arms beside her. He felt as though it was only now, that very moment, that this woman had died. Then he turned round, found his way to the door and across the echoing passage, and re-entered the laboratory they had left earlier. Dr Adler followed silently, locking the door behind him.

Fridolin went over to the wash-basin. "May I?" he said and washed his hands thoroughly with soap and lysol. Meanwhile Dr Adler seemed eager to resume his interrupted work without delay. He had switched his light on again, adjusted the micrometer and was peering into the microscope. When Fridolin came over to take his leave, he was already engrossed in his work.

"Do you want to have a look at the culture?" he asked.

"What for?" asked Fridolin absently.

"Well, to satisfy your conscience," replied Dr Adler,—as though he were taking it as understood that the purpose of Fridolin's visit had been medical and scientific.

"Can you interpret it?" he asked while Fridolin looked into the microscope. "It's a fairly recent colour-contrastive method."

Fridolin nodded without removing his eye from the microscope. "Perfect, really," he remarked, "a splendid colour picture, you might say."

And he enquired about various details the new technique involved.

Dr Adler gave him the information he required and

Fridolin remarked that the novel technique might well prove very useful in some work he was planning for the near future. He asked if he might come again tomorrow or the next day to seek further information.

"Always pleased to be of service," said Dr Adler, and accompanied Fridolin along the echoing flag-stones to the main door, which meanwhile had been locked, and opened it with his own key.

"You are staying on?" asked Fridolin.

"But of course," replied Dr Adler, "this is by far the best time to work—from about midnight until morning. At least one is reasonably safe from inter-ruptions."

"Quite so," said Fridolin with a quiet, slightly guilty smile.

Dr Adler laid his hand reassuringly on Fridolin's arm, then he asked with a certain diffidence: "Well—was it she?"

Fridolin hesitated a moment, then nodded silently, and was scarcely conscious that this affirmation might quite possibly be untrue. For whether or not the woman now lying in the mortuary was the one whom twenty-four hours earlier he had held naked in his arms, to the wild accompaniment of Nightingale's piano, or whether she was really a complete stranger, of one thing he was absolutely certain. Even if the woman he was looking for, had desired and for an hour perhaps loved were still alive, and regardless of how she continued to conduct her life, what lay be-hind him in that vaulted room—in the gloom of flick-ering gas-lamps, a shadow among shades, as dark, meaningless and devoid of mystery as they,—could now mean nothing to him but the pale corpse of the previous night, destined irrevocably for decay.

VII

He hurried home through the dark deserted streets, and a few minutes later, having undressed in his consulting-room as he had done twenty-four hours earlier, he entered the marital bedroom as quietly as possible.

He could hear Albertine's calm regular breathing and see the outline of her head silhouetted against the soft pillow. A feeling of tenderness and of security he had not expected overwhelmed him. And he resolved to tell her the whole story of the previous night quite soon, perhaps even tomorrow, but as if everything he had experienced had only been a dream—and then, when she had felt and acknowledged the insignificance of his adventure, he would confess that it had indeed been real. Real? he asked himself—, and at that moment became aware of something very close to Albertine's face on the other pillow, on *his* pillow, something dark and quite distinct, like the shadowy outline of a human face. His heart stood still for an instant until he grasped the situation, and reaching out he seized the mask he had worn the previous night, which evidently had slipped out without his noticing that morning as he rolled up his costume, and which the chambermaid or even Albertine herself must then have found. So he could scarcely doubt that after this discovery Albertine must suspect something, and conceivably worse things than had actually happened. Yet the way she had chosen to let him know this, the idea of laying the dark mask out on the pillow next to her, as if to represent his, her husband's face, which had become a riddle to her, this witty, almost light-hearted approach, which seemed to contain both a mild warning and a willingness to forgive, gave Fridolin reason to hope that, remembering her own dream, she would be disposed not to take whatever might have happened all that seriously. But then suddenly, feeling utterly exhausted, Fridolin let the mask slip to the floor and to his own surprise broke into loud, heart-rending sobs, then sank down beside the bed and wept quietly into the pillow.

A few seconds later he felt a soft hand stroking his hair. He raised his head and from the bottom of his heart cried: "I will tell you everything."

At first she gently raised her hand as if to prevent him, but he seized it and held it in his own, looking up at her both questioning and pleading with her, and so she nodded her consent and he began.

By the time Fridolin had ended the first grey light of dawn was coming through the curtains. Albertine had not once interrupted him with curious or impatient questions. She seemed to sense that he was neither able nor willing to conceal anything from her. She lay there quietly, her hands behind her neck, and remained silent a long time after Fridolin had finished. At last—he had been lying stretched out by her side—he bent over her and, gazing into her impassive face and large bright eyes, in which the day now seemed to be dawning too, asked hesitantly yet full of hope: "What should we do, Albertine?"

She smiled, and after hesitating briefly answered: "I think we should be grateful to fate that we have safely emerged from these adventures—both from the real ones and from those we dreamed about."

"Are you quite sure of that?" he asked.

"As sure as I am of my sense that neither the reality of a single night, nor even of a person's entire life can be equated with the full truth about his innermost being.

"And no dream," he sighed quietly, "is altogether a dream." She took his head in both her hands and pillowed it tenderly against her breast. "Now we are truly awake," she said, "at least for a good while." He wanted to add: forever, but before he had a chance to speak, she laid a finger on his lips and whispered as though to herself: "Never enquire into the future."

And so they both lay there in silence, both dozing now and then, yet dreamlessly close to one another—until, as every morning at seven, there was a knock upon the bedroom door and, with the usual noises from the street, a triumphant sunbeam coming in between the curtains, and a child's gay laughter from the adjacent room, another day began.